Ulterior
Motives

by David Garnett

Harcourt, Brace & World, Inc., New York

First American edition 1967
Library of Congress Catalog Card Number: 67-10761
Printed in the United States of America

To Harold Hobson
In gratitude for a friendship
begun in 1898

Ulterior Motives

1

In the room looking over the terrace into the park beyond and opening onto it through three French windows, the Beaumont family was having a thoroughly English breakfast, as was usual in the Château de Berri. Though they were bilingual, except for Leela, who, being Russian, had an equally imperfect command of the niceties of French and English, they talked English, as was usual.

"For how long shall we have to endure this army friend of Winston's?" asked Pash.

"The boy did not say in his telegram how long," replied Leela. "But as Captain Kitson is driving Winston here, I assumed he would stay the night and then go on to wherever he is going."

"Winston is capable of having asked him to stay for a month," said Pash.

Her father, first putting up his hand to reassure Proust, the cat, on his shoulder, looked up from *The Times* and then went back to it. It was always yesterday's *Times*, but no one would have suspected it from St. Clair's attitude.

"I have put him in the Pink Room," said Leela.

"More coffee, please," said Alamein, passing her big bowl. Her father put aside *The Times*, reassured Proust with a caress, and refilled it for her.

"It's not that I object to all of Winston's friends as individuals," said Pash tolerantly. "I mean if Winston

3

weren't here, or if he didn't like them, it wouldn't be so hellish having his friends in the house. It's the combination of Winston's hero worship and the embarrassed and pointless object of it, shivering with outraged modesty, or glowing with budding vanity, which is so frightful." Pash was enjoying her explanation and preparing to enlarge upon it.

"Winston has such a warm enthusiastic nature, and I am sure his friends love him all the better because of it," said Leela. There was a silence. Then Pash went on:

"The hero worship is bound to be particularly appalling with this army friend. We shall hear how Captain Kitson was the bravest of the brave in Cyprus with the most shy-making details. I am willing to bet that he risked his life to save a little Turkish girl from a time bomb. All his medals and mentions in dispatches will be gone into and trumpeted to us at breakfast, dinner, lunch, and tea. . . ." Pash went into a peal of laughter at the prospect.

"Pass the honey," said Alamein. It was passed.

"Why the Pink Room?" asked Pash suddenly.

"It has the view into the garden. Also a washbasin and hot water," replied Leela.

"Do we really want Winston's army friend to overlook us every time we go for a stroll in the garden?" asked Pash. St. Clair folded *The Times* and began doing the crossword puzzle on the back.

"I hope you don't drive him away after one night under the same roof with you, Pash. I rather like having a strange man in the house," said Alamein, speaking with her mouth full. St. Clair looked up with interest at his younger daughter, and Proust deliberately leapt down to the floor. "There will be time for the strangeness to wear off," St. Clair drawled in his invariably slow and dreamy

4

voice. "Because I invited Captain Kitson to stay here for a week or ten days."

His words were a surprise.

"Oh Christ!" exclaimed Pash, getting up from the table and leaving the room. Alamein followed her sister after picking out a couple of the largest strawberries from a plate on the sideboard. Proust leapt up onto St. Clair's lap and then onto his shoulder. Leela, after waiting for a minute in silence, asked:

"Do you think Pash hates to have young men coming here because of me? Because I am an embarrassment to you all and cannot be explained?"

St. Clair smashed his *Times* onto the table, and Proust leapt down again. But even when irritated, the master of the house spoke in a slow drawl. "Hell take you women. Such god-damned fools. Why do I have to live with such cretins?"

Leela gazed at him bleakly, balancing herself on the edge of a quarrel. "I don't know," she said almost tearfully.

"Oh yes, you do," growled St. Clair. Leela lifted her eyes to his.

"Come here," he ordered, angry but concupiscent. Five minutes later he shook off her embraces, got out of his chair, picked Proust off the floor, gathered up *The Times*, and went to his study. Very soon the typewriter began clacking vigorously. St. Clair was an author.

Rollo Kitson was in the driving seat; Winston Beaumont beside him. Both were big men in goggles and white helmets who sped over the fertile plains of France. But in spite of identical goggles and helmets they did not resemble each other. Vast expanses of underdone beef complexion and a crisp fair mustache were visible above the

5

steering wheel; a dusky nectarine's softer cheek on the left hand. For it was a right-hand-drive English car—an MG.

The younger man held a map open on his knees, but he did not look at it. It was hard to say why he held it, except that his companion had asked him to map-read, for he knew the roads of that part of France by heart.

"I think you'll like Pash. She's much the most conventional of us," he said. "And of course she's quite intelligent too."

"Pash? Which one is that?"

"Pasionaria, my elder sister—named after the Communist heroine of the Spanish Civil War. You see, my mother was tremendously anti-fascist, and that's how we all got our names."

Captain Kitson remembered that he had heard all this before as his young admirer recited: "Pasionaria, Winston, Alamein."

Pasionaria's intelligence did not predispose him in her favor but prompted the question:

"What sort of an intelligence?"

"Probing. She tries to dig out and to drag out everything which would be better left covered up. In a way she's rather like our Aunt Fidèle, though of course Aunt Fidèle is no blood relation."

"I don't seem to have heard of that one," Captain Kitson muttered in a tone which might have been either banter or an amiable resignation to boredom.

"*La tante* Fidèle is like someone out of the first volume of Proust's *À la Recherche du Temps Perdu*. She is always explaining to all and sundry just why it is impossible for her to visit us." Winston paused, giving his companion the opportunity to ask why—but when he said nothing, he continued:

6

"It is because of *cette femme:* that is to say, Leela—whom she regards as an immoral woman. Whenever I meet *ma tante* Fidèle, wherever she may be and whoever may be present, she at once begins to explain, all over again. So we all avoid her like the plague.

"Pash retaliates by explaining to Aunt Fidèle's friends that she won't visit her as she objects to criticisms of her father. 'I will never be disloyal!' she proclaims and is particularly proud of having invented that ridiculous phrase and of the whole stunt.

"The result is that our uncle and our cousins come to see us quite a lot and that we never go and see them. It is a good arrangement, as we live in the château and they live in a poky little house in a side street, with my uncle's surgery in the front room. As a matter of fact, Aunt Fidèle and the priest are the only people who have worked up this thing about Leela."

"Rather tough for her, not being able to marry your father," said Captain Kitson with unexpected chivalry.

"It doesn't make any difference. She could only marry him if she were a divorced woman, and neither Aunt Fidèle nor the priest recognizes divorce. In fact, they think remarriage after divorce is a lot worse than living in sin. *L'oncle* Mathieu—that's Doctor Robert—my mother's half-brother—always makes a point of being very chummy with Leela, and luckily he and Yseult, his daughter, think that Aunt Fidèle is a museum piece."

Rollo Kitson grunted and tugged at his mustache. He saw it was going to be a bit of a strain staying for a fortnight—yet a fortnight it would have to be, because Myrna Lorriner had made it clear that she could not have him until the end of the first week in July.

Actually he didn't find it a strain, though there were odd moments.

7

On the very first day, when the whole family was present, Rollo had, in speaking to Leela, referred to his host as "Mr. Beaumont."

"De Beaumont, me boy," St. Clair corrected in his sleepy drawl. Rollo gaped, and St. Clair went on: "On coming to live in France I decided to restore the 'de,' which was of course used by my Norman French-speaking ancestors. So I am known by all my neighbors as De Beaumont and I always insist on the use of the particle while I am in France. It was dropped in England during the fifteenth century, but it has always been preserved by the French branch. I trust you agree that it was the right thing to restore it."

"Absolutely," murmured Rollo, awe-struck.

"Since we are on the subject, you should tell Captain Kitson that your grandfather's name was actually the German Baumann," said Pash witheringly.

"I never disguise it," said St. Clair. "There it is in the family tree: Baumann. Our branch of the Beaumonts, or De Beaumonts, as one must properly call them, went over to Germany and were engaged in commerce in the early nineteenth century. For commercial reasons they called themselves Baumann—they didn't translate the name into Schönberg I'm glad to say, but used a name which sounded like Beaumont—Baumann. My father, who was born and brought up in England, went back to our old family name of Beaumont in 1914, when he was naturally anxious to get rid of any suspicion of association with the Hun."

"He sold cheap alarm clocks and junk imported from Germany, so it was natural that he should be supposed to be descended from Attila," said Pash.

Alamein gave a snort, which was disregarded by her father.

8

"A liveryman of the City of London and master of the Shoe-Horn Makers Company," said St. Clair dreamily.

"I thought that was his brother Isadore," said Pash.

"Quite right. As I was about to say, his half-brother, my uncle Sir Isadore, was a distinguished merchant in the City."

"Jewish," said Pash.

"My half-uncle's mother was a Jewess. I hope there is no anti-Semite at this table," said St. Clair portentously.

Pash laughed and got up and went out of the room with a contemptuous lower lip thrust out. Her father watched her departure quizzically; then he seemed to dismiss her from his mind. "Proust, behave yourself," he interjected as the big tomcat on his shoulders stood up and dug in his claws.

"The arms of our branch of the family are or, a lion azure within an orle of fleur-de-lis or on a ground azure. I don't know whether you value heraldry as I do, Captain Kitson, but I have always been proud that in my shield I bear the golden fleur-de-lis of *la belle France* on the ground azure, the arms of the royal family of the Bourbons."

"Hum," said Rollo.

"I feel it most gratifying because of having married into the old French aristocracy."

"Oh, I see," said Rollo, and began knocking his pipe out noisily on the fender and then feeling for his pouch to refill it. When he looked round he saw that Leela, Alamein, and Winston had left the room.

Rollo filled his pipe, lit it, and pulled at it thoughtfully, looking at Mr. de Beaumont with distrust.

I don't suppose I shall get a bean out of the old Jew, he reflected pessimistically. The older man had begun again, and was saying:

9

". . . a companion of Baldwin, Count of Flanders and prominent as an organizer of the sixth Crusade. The arms of my late wife, Marie-Thérèse, chatelaine Du Bartas, which I bear in party with those of De Beaumont, are therefore argent and sable, with six luces haurient sable and argent countercharged."

Rollo shook his head from side to side. His pipe had gone out; he probed it with a match and relit it. But his host was looking at him with astonishment.

"Is there anything which leads you to doubt what I am saying?" he asked severely, recalling Rollo to the reality of his position.

"Oh no, not at all. Can't get this pipe to draw. Must look for a feather when I go out."

"And what do you say you are, Captain Kitson?"

Rollo hadn't said what he was and seemed somewhat surprised. He thought about it and then replied:

"Well you might call me a financier, Mr. de Beaumont."

"That's just what we want. In fact, it is most opportune. Not for me—but for my nephew, or, rather, my brother-in-law's nephew. He's looking for a financier. He actually tried to get me to put up money. In fact, I may if the thing is being properly managed."

"Just what sort of business does he want financed?" asked Rollo.

"We'll get him over and he can tell you all about it. I deal with the truths of the imagination. I am a writer of fiction. Amadeo is a scientist making plans for building a city on the moon."

St. Clair rose, and remarking: "Come along, Proust, we must get back to our typing," left the room with Proust standing up and balanced on his left shoulder.

———

10

Leela came into the room where Winston was looking disconsolately out of the window.

"I wish you would ask Pasionaria not to gird at St. Clair all the time," she said, taking him by the hand. "I'm sure she would listen to you."

"I think it is better that she should gird at him," said Winston without either looking at her or trying to move his hand away.

"Oh no, you don't. You know it is useless and that it upsets everyone—and that there is no reason for it."

"Pash hates it when St. Clair talks buncombe."

"What's that?"

"Well you know she hates it."

"No, what does that word mean—buncombe?"

"A polite word for balls. A bit old-fashioned—Victorian." She pulled at his hand and murmured:

"You are such a help, Winston. I don't know what I should do if I couldn't talk to you sometimes. Pasionaria is so difficult, and Alamein always behaves as though there weren't any problems in life. Nothing gets me down more than cheery optimism. And Pasionaria is a problem. It is almost impossible to help her."

"She's of age. She doesn't want help. She's old enough to look after herself."

"None of us are as old as that, Winston. Least of all St. Clair."

This time it was Winston who pulled Leela's hand, and as she bent down, put his other arm round her neck and gave her a kiss of encouragement.

At that moment Pash was sunk deep in a chair and saying to Alamein in tones of profound despair:

"Why should we have a circus clown for our father?" She spoke in French, but used the word clown, which is French as well as English.

11

"A clown?" repeated Alamein.

"A buffoon who can be relied on to put on a clown's turn when it is least wanted. He is not a bad man; he's not even really stupid. But he has an infallible sense of knowing when and how to bitch everything up. He can't help it. Blast him. Damn his eyes. He *would* make us appear the most ghastly eccentric snobs just when the first wildly attractive man comes into the house."

"I suppose it is really a good thing," said Alamein.

Pasionaria clasped and unclasped her hands. "A good thing! Why it is an agony to sit through."

"Yes, it is an agony all right," agreed Alamein. "But it is a good thing because if Captain Kitson is an ordinary conventional idiot, it will scare him off. And if he's intelligent enough he won't mind."

"I think he is an ordinary conventional idiot," said Pash. "But that is no reason for wanting to lose him."

"I think you are foul beyond words," exclaimed Alamein.

"And I think you are a completely unrealistic little idealist and, what's more, the kind of chicken-headedness you stand for appears to me positively nauseating."

"I simply cannot understand thinking a man attractive when you don't know the first thing about him," said Alamein.

"You don't know the first thing about anything, least of all your own feelings. It is really a waste of time talking to you," said Pasionaria.

Pasionaria was the unhappy member of a happy household.

She was five years older than Alamein—old enough to have a vivid memory of her mother and to hate her father for having so easily consoled himself after her death with such an inferior contemptible creature as Leela. She hated her father for his grandiose speeches, despised his origins, was nauseated by his lies. She identified herself with her mother's aristocratic family; longed to escape from St. Clair's rackety bohemian world of make-believe into her own daydream world every bit as unreal—a world inhabited by titled and fashionable people to which only respectable, well-born, and *bien-pensant* ladies and gentlemen were admitted. She believed that if only her poor deluded mother had not picked up a lot of crazy ideas and married an imposter, that was the world she would have been born to ornament. Instead of which, she was saddled with the absurd name of a Communist heroine, living with an impossible, unpresentable father and his sloppy mistress and with a romantic younger sister as her companion. Eighteen months previously she had escaped from home to a job in an architect's office. But she had allowed herself to be seduced by her employer, had become pregnant, and had been forced to return home after having an abortion. Since then she had despised herself nearly as much as she despised the other members of her family.

Only her uncle, Dr. Robert, knew of this episode in her life, and she could rely on him never to refer to it. She had gone to consult him in a panic when she had a hemorrhage after the operation was over.

Pasionaria was proud, and her life seemed to her to bring nothing but humiliation; it was indeed humiliating to be a woman and to depend on exciting and exploiting the sexual appetite of a man. But her pride led her to face facts: which was to see everything in life in its crudest colors. She would have liked to tear away all the pretenses, to force people to admit that all was lust and lies and appetite and avarice.

But even that consolation was denied to her pride,

13

for she knew that hypocrisy was essential for a woman to succeed and that the first step toward success was in catching a rich man. And for that, sweetness, modesty, and innocence were requisite. Captain Kitson's visit was an opportunity to display them.

Rollo's two-seater was made to carry four so that Winston and his sisters could show him the ruins of Château Bartas, which had been built by their ancestors in the fourteenth century. Alamein sat on Pasionaria's lap, and Winston, with his feet in the trunk, clung to the framework of the folded top. Alamein had never seen Rollo's face so close; it really was enormous and exactly the color of underdone cold beef, and the short hairs of his mustache and the eyelashes and eyebrows were the color of yellow oat straw, though the fair hair of his head was more like weathered wheat straw, with even a touch of very pale brown in it. She looked at the face several times, but he never took his eyes off the road. It seemed to her rather frightful that the owner of that face was alive and thinking his own thoughts and that he had already formed an impression of her.

At Bartas-les-Pierres they bathed in the moat, listened to the frogs croaking in chorus, paraded the village, and Winston took photographs of Alamein and Rollo holding out their arms to each other in the ruins of the castle. Though she did not realize it herself, it was Alamein's day. Pasionaria did, and gave herself up to encouraging her little sister. Meanwhile she wondered whether Captain Kitson thought she was too dark, too short, too French. Alamein was two inches taller than she; her hair was light brown instead of black, her eyes a green hazel instead of dark, and she had no tiny dark hairs on her upper lip, foreshadowing a mustache.

But she remained cool and was gaily jocular, encourag-

14

ing the flirtation but showing no inclination to take part in it.

That evening Rollo and the two sisters sat in the garden, and Alamein talked, asking questions about Winston's life in the army. Pasionaria suspected that Rollo found Winston a bore and did not commit herself. Rollo cleaned his pipe very thoroughly with the feather he had found on their outing, filled it carefully, lit it, and listened, and once or twice took it out of his mouth to make a non-committal remark, or to agree with what Alamein said. Then Winston came out and suggested that they come in and play poker.

Rollo played carefully and won fifteen francs.

Next morning Leela announced that St. Clair's brother-in-law, Dr. Robert, was coming to see them, bringing his daughter, Yseult, and his nephew, Amadeo Severin, who was half Italian. "The poor child is an orphan and brought up by his uncle in Venice," she said.

"I am afraid you must find all these relations of ours very confusing," said Pasionaria with a warm smile. But Rollo, who was good at puzzles, had fathomed the connections of the De Beaumont family and replied:

"Yseult is your cousin or half-cousin, if there is such a word, but Amadeo Severin is not a blood relation of yours at all. Am I right, Pash?"

Pasionaria clapped her hands in high delight. "Oh, how clever you are. You see, l'oncle Mathieu—that is, Dr. Robert—was our mother's younger half-brother, and his father, the General, also married a second time, so that our uncle had a half-sister with no Du Bartas blood at all—poor creature." The last words were said in a sparkling comic aside. "So she married a Venetian called Severin. Amadeo is Yseult's cousin but not ours, which is a fearful pity, because he is the only genius in the family."

15

"Hum," said Rollo.

"He is quite, quite certain to end up as a multimillion-aire because he has invented all the comforts one will want for space travel," said Pasionaria, determined not to be discouraged.

Rollo laughed, a warm hearty laugh that made Pasionaria feel more contented.

"Space Travel Accessories Limited. No reason why not," he said aloud, and then thought to himself: If one held the early patents one could probably sell out to the big shots who have the resources to deal with space travel and would not want the threat of legal actions. Space travel had possibilities. Pasionaria stretched her arms wide, and then managed to lead Rollo Kitson out into the garden. When they were alone together she looked at him confidingly and said:

"I hope you'll forgive me, Captain Kitson, if I tell you how the land lies. Of course in secret. You see, although Amadeo has never declared himself, I can see that he is very much attracted by Alamein. She is such a child that she hasn't realized it, but I have, and I do hope it will come to something in time. It is a terribly suitable match. But Amadeo would never do anything until he has had one of his inventions taken up. Alamein adores him, but she is a complete child."

Rollo jerked his head to one side to show his under-standing of the subtleties of the situation. Then he took his pipe out of his mouth, knocked it out on his heel, and said:

"Thank you very much, Pash, for telling me. I feel you are taking me into the family and I appreciate it. Thanks a lot."

They returned to the house with Pasionaria treading on air—Captain Kitson had twice called her Pash—and found that the Roberts and Amadeo had just arrived.

The genius of the family was not very Italian looking: he was fair, with gray-blue eyes, rosy cheeks, and with a rather dreamy faraway expression. He spoke English perfectly.

Rollo asked him what he was inventing, and Amadeo, smiling slightly, said that he had stopped inventing things until he could get some of his existing inventions taken up.

"I'm looking for money," he said, and somehow the twinkle in his eye was not that of a man who is really looking for money.

"I'm a financier," said Rollo. "We might do business."

"I don't suppose for a moment that you will be attracted by my inventions. Financiers never are. You see, I am interested in what I call telefaction: that is, making things or doing things at a distance by a new method of the transmission of power, with remote control and fully automatic machinery."

"What is new about it?" asked Rollo.

"Well, really my discovery was in two parts. The first is that the twin crystals of a particular mineral have unique electrical properties. That is to say, that an electric current passing through one of the twins induces an electric current of the opposite sign in the other, no matter how far they are apart. Of course I have only actually tried them on the earth. But I believe that it is true for far greater distances. This discovery has little practical value except in telephony, which I haven't had time to work at. Because while doing some quite different experiments, I hit on what I call the "multiplier." That is a system by which under certain circumstances a minute electric current can be made to act as a guide, inducing or focusing a powerful one. Actually it is minute electric charges which explain why lightning strikes where it does, which

17

is a comparable phenomenon in static electricity. But my two discoveries, used together, enable me to transmit power to any distance with practically no wastage. It is not a beam like the "death ray"—which is effective for about half a mile or so, but which can't be pinpointed—but what I can only call an individual crystalline affinity and which can be pinpointed at wherever you site your receiver twin."

Rollo nodded. He hadn't the vaguest notion whether what Severin had said made sense or was cuckoo. Get him back to earth.

"What do you plan to use it for?"

"Making anything that is wanted. The obvious use is in the transmission of power from generating stations to wherever power is wanted. It means that electricity can be generated wherever it is most economical to do so and transmitted to wherever it is wanted without a grid of cables and practically without wastage. But the new uses to which it can be put are chiefly in cybernetics: particularly in doing things where it is difficult for man to work. For example, drilling for oil at the bottom of the sea. You wouldn't need a rig and a floating platform. I have also been wondering about extracting minerals from active volcanoes in the Andes."

"Hum," said Rollo. It sounded to him as though one might lose a lot of money that way. "What have you actually done?" he asked.

"Well, very little. I need millions to try it out fully. But by substituting an electric motor for the gasoline engine I can run a car off the mains."

"Be up against the oil companies," said Rollo.

"And since there is always more money available for armaments, I have worked out the detailed plans of a demonstration tank operated by remote control from anywhere you choose on earth. It is only a question of money to make a fully equipped tank corps as part of a fully automatic army corps which could be operated as part of an invasion of, let's say, Russia, or, if you prefer, the United States, from a base in New Zealand. But although that has never been done, it is already quite out of date. The project which interests me far more than any of these armament toys is to build a fully equipped city on the moon, ready for the first human beings to take up residence. It is quite possible, but the variables run into billions. Actually, of course, they will be immensely reduced and brought into the range of the possible by trial and error."

Rollo smacked his great palms together and laughed. He felt a bit shaken by what Amadeo had said, but it was obvious that he was on to a big thing. A much bigger thing than he had ever dreamed of. He took his pipe out of his pocket, filled it, and laughed again as he pressed the mixture down into the bowl. Then he lit it and said:

"I hope we can do business. It sounds just up my street."

"What are you two boobies conspiring about?" asked Alamein, coming up and putting her hand on the back of the chair on which Rollo was sitting. He turned his head to look at her.

"I think you may be able to give me some help here," he said. Their eyes met, and a sudden thrill of unknown excitement went through Alamein. What on earth was coming?

When Rollo had said "You may be able to give me some help," he was thinking that if anyone could persuade Mr. de Beaumont to invest a large sum in Telefaction Limited, it would be his lovely young daughter. But since she was expecting an explanation of the words, he said:

19

"Do you believe in that chap?" and nodded his head sagely at Amadeo. "Is he as good as his word? Has he ever let you down?"

Alamein stared first at one of the two men and then at the other, feeling supremely proud and happy.

"Everyone knows that he is a genius. Well, I will add that he is completely reliable. If he tells you that he can light a box of matches on the moon, he says it not as something to boast of, but as something which he happens to know is true. You can believe without the faintest shadow of doubt that he can light a box of matches on the moon."

"I can't light matches on the moon; I never shall be able to light *matches* there," said Amadeo.

They laughed, and Alamein went on. "That is typical. He can't light matches. But I am sure he can light something."

"Given time I could certainly produce an electric arc on the moon," said Amadeo. "It might not be very good for lighting your pipe, Mr. Kitson, but it would weld steel or light up a street."

"Fair enough. That's just what I wanted to know, Alamein; now we can go places."

Captain Kitson had never called her by her Christian name before!

Alamein flushed with excitement. "Go places? Do you mean to the moon?" she asked.

Rollo laughed. "Well we'll get Telefaction Limited set up on earth first." Suddenly his eyes clouded. "Do you favor setting up the company in London or in Paris?" he asked.

"What about Rome?" said Amadeo.

"My father says that Switzerland is the only capitalist paradise left," said Alamein.

20

"What about the moon? Have you thought of registering our company there?" said Amadeo, and gave a little giggle.

"Ha! Ha!" laughed Rollo. "Hum," he added, sucking at his pipe. Amadeo's suggestion had left him a little uncomfortable.

And the rosy-cheeked young Italian's next remark did not dispel his uneasiness.

"You know, I've often thought that the moon would be much the best base from which to carry out telefaction operations on the earth."

"Come on, we're going bathing before lunch; pile into the cars," cried Pasionaria, coming to join them.

2

Under the poplars bunched on high with mistletoe, between the dark green alleys ran the river: a narrow enough stream in spite of its great name. At moments it spread out to contain a large pool of lily pads; in a clearer portion, where the sunlight broke through a gap in the trees, was the *lavoir*, a long open building with a concrete floor under a slate roof where a few women were to be found beating and sousing their washing on most mornings of the week. While they worked a strand of dirty opaque water entered the stream and a flow of gossip was carried away by the air. Round a bend, upstream, was a hatch: the river was deeper there, and in the green gloom of summer the De Beaumont family made it their bathing place, with a springboard jutting from the bank and a diving stage with one board two meters above the water and an upper one three meters. Comfreys fringed the bank; purple loosestrife and meadowsweet grew high on the plashy verges.

During the summer the girls were always bathing. Before breakfast Pash and Alamein would bicycle the kilometer separating the château from the river. In the afternoon they would pile into the old Renault and drive there. At night they would suddenly decide on a dip before bed, diving from the obscure platform into the unseen darkness of the water below.

During the fortnight that Captain Kitson stayed with

them they pressed his smart MG into service for transport. On this occasion Rollo and Amadeo drove in it with Alamein clinging on behind, while Pash drove Yseult, *l'oncle* Mathieu, and Winston in the Renault.

The girls were polished divers, but the energy of Dr. Robert was astounding. He was bald, he was fifty, but he did half a dozen running forward somersaults from the springboard and back somersaults from the three-meter board and lovely falling dives, holding his body absolutely stiff and straight. Rollo, the largest and most muscular of all the figures, was an indifferent diver; he was unable to prevent himself kicking up his legs behind.

Feeling aware of his lack of skill, he stood sunning himself and admiring the scene. Amadeo paused to speak to him, and Rollo said: "This reminds me of one of those lovely Renoir paintings."

Amadeo pulled a face. "More like a Corot. My cousins aren't like Renoir girls."

Rollo did not dispute the point; he was content to have made his number as a lover of French art and he was gratified to hear his remark being translated to Dr. Robert, who, unlike the others, was not completely bilingual.

Next moment the doctor had called out: "*Votre Monsieur Kitson trouve que vous ressemblez aux modèles de Renoir.*"

Shrieks of indignation arose from Pasionaria and Yseult. "I have a waist of fifty-four centimeters," exclaimed Yseult.

That evening, before she got into bed, Alamein inspected her naked body carefully in the cheval glass and was not displeased with what she saw. Her expression was fierce and reckless.

"Why should I let Pash call me sentimental and chicken-headed? I'm not in love, but why shouldn't I experiment? E. M. Forster says that love is of the body. Rollo's got a splendid body. I can have him if I want to. Why not?" She imagined Rollo standing beside her, his big hands stroking her breasts. Then he was kneeling in front of her, holding her round the waist, burying his head and kissing her like the man in that marble group by the German sculptor Fritz Klimsch that Winston had put up on his wall and that Pash had said she had thrown away, and which had afterward been found in her chest of drawers.

Alamein put on her pajamas, turned out the light, and jumped into bed, hoping to give herself up to the sensuality of further daydreams, but she slipped almost at once into a dreamless sleep. Next morning she remembered her decision to take Rollo as her lover as an experiment and felt ashamed. "And yet? Who knows? Am I just a chicken-headed little fool?" she asked herself.

They went bathing again, and she looked carefully at Rollo. He was clumsy. But then he was so big, and she thought that there is a clumsiness which is inseparable from all big animals such as bulls and Newfoundland dogs. She would have preferred a lover like a leopard. But probably she was being chicken-headed not to take what was there instead of dreaming about the impossible. The perfectionist got nothing and ended up as an old maid.

That evening Rollo wondered whether perhaps there was not a rival, and a dangerous one, nosing round Severin's invention.

Dr. Robert, Amadeo, and Yseult came over to dinner bringing with them an English visitor: Sir Samuel Tonson, whom they all called Sam. He was a man of about fifty,

24

tall, stooping, a little paunchy, with a bald head, deep-blue eyes, and a mustache which did not hide his moist red lips.

The new arrival was greeted with enthusiasm by the ladies of the household, who kissed him, exclaimed that he was looking tired, and begged him to stay for a long while with their uncle. All this was rather peculiar, because it soon came out that they had only met Sir Sam once before, when he had spent a couple of days with Dr. Robert.

Rollo noticed that St. Clair had put the ribbon of the Legion of Honor in his buttonhole and that he treated his visitor with marked cordiality and respect—a respect which, to Rollo's surprise, was obviously returned.

"How is your new book going and what is the subject?" Sir Sam asked.

St. Clair nodded his head meditatively, opened his mouth widely, and said very slowly, savoring each word: "Well, when I taught Marcel Proust to write French . . ." But he paused so long, allowing this remarkable exordium to soak in, that Rollo asked in a puzzled voice: "I always thought Proust was French."

St. Clair turned to Rollo and said in tones of perfect courtesy but still drawling out his words one by one:

"You are mistaken, Captain Kitson. Proust's ancestry is pure British. He was born in the Temple, and I like to think that he has Hodge's blood in his veins, though it would be difficult to construct a pedigree. But what Hodge was to Johnson Proust is to me, and I would use the same words about him." Then leaving Rollo baffled and effectively excluded from the conversation, he continued, addressing himself to Sir Sam, in slow explanation:

"Marcel Proust was searching for a style, and I en-

25

abled him to find what he was looking for simply by substituting *The Wings of the Dove* for *The Stones of Venice* as his bedside reading. I didn't even do it intentionally. You see, at seventeen I worshiped James and had no use for Ruskin, and I had just met Proust, who was madly in love with me. I was often in his bedroom and left my books there—and that is how Proust got those wonderfully long involved sentences which have so enriched French prose."

"Fascinating," said Sir Sam.

"Unfortunately I neglected to educate myself in a corresponding manner." St. Clair paused, but reassured by his visitor's obvious interest he continued: "Well now I have done it. It needed courage, I can tell you, at my age to fling Flaubert out of the window, to scrub out Stendhal, and jettison James. . . ."

"I hope you are not going to model your style on *Finnegans Wake*," said Sir Sam.

"No. Not Joyce. Not Gertrude, I am even happier to say. Not dear old Ernest, thank God. But Djuna. Djuna gave me the clue, and that was all I needed. Djuna is my port of departure."

"And the subject?" asked Sir Sam.

"I would call it the dilemma of victory. When the Polynesian warrior kills his enemy, he eats him and becomes possessed of his spirit. Western man does the same. We conquer the Germans and then we become them. This has happened to France, and I speak as a Frenchman. . . ."

"And I also speak as a Frenchman, per'aps even a more authentic specimen," said Dr. Robert, choosing his words with difficulty and speaking in English only out of politeness to Rollo.

"It is not the victory which was not ours: we did not

conquer 'eem. It is not the cannibalism. It is the nature of the German. In 1870 'e left us the legacy of revenge and of militarism—what you call 'my country, right or wrong.' After 1918 it was the legacy of fear, because we 'ad been almost bled to death because of our bad generals, and after 1940 it is one of spiritual corruption. If you want to find Nazis today, you must look for them in France."

"That is what I was explaining is the theme of the book I have just sent to the publisher," said St. Clair. "France is today almost a dictatorship, a fascist state in which torture goes unpunished. And the dilemma my hero faces is how man can win the battle for survival without losing what he fought for."

"A magnificent, a splendid and noble subject. But is Djuna Barnes exactly the medium? I find her luxuriant metaphors and her rich language almost incomprehensible," said Sir Sam.

"You see, I have written my new novel in French. And Djuna gives my French exactly the shade I need. It makes it positively iridescent, like a woman's wig. No one has ever written French like mine—not even Mallarmé. My book will cause a tremendous excitement. . . ." St. Clair paused, and abandoned the subject of style. Then his eye lit up and, nodding meditatively, he drawled: "When I last dined with the General, I asked him whether he would grow a Hitlerian lock of hair and adopt a toothbrush mustache. But I don't think he understood why I asked."

"*Impayable*," murmured Dr. Robert.

But St. Clair's daughters had grown restive.

"I suspect you already know Captain Kitson. You must have met him in the City of London, since, like you, he is a financier," said Pash, turning to Sir Sam. She was hoping to find out something about Rollo.

27

"No, Pash. I'm not a financier; I'm a tycoon," replied Sir Sam with a gentleness of manner that was habitual. "And am I to understand, Mr. Kitson, that you are a banker?"

"No, sir. I am more like a company promoter."

Sir Sam winced a little at the "sir," laughed, and turned back to talk to the girls. However, Leela had a question.

"I know what a financier is. He is a man with millions of money. But what is a tycoon, Sam?"

"A tycoon is an autocrat of industry. I am the autocrat of the computer industry and I spend my life planning to put millions of men out of work forever, though of course I always deny that cybernetics—that is, computers directing automation—will lead to any unemployment at all. But our desire to bring all manual work to an end is what Amadeo and I have in common." There was a silence. Then Sir Sam turned to Rollo and asked: "Would the future of those men worry you if you were me, Mr. Kitson?"

"I shouldn't lose any sleep thinking about them, sir," said Rollo with a laugh.

"Well, Severin and I do. We were sitting up with Mathieu here to all hours last night discussing the solution to the problem."

"There aren't any solutions to those sorts of problems," said St. Clair suddenly. "Much better recognize it straight away. My poor wife never did and was always in a hopeless tangle. Lived and died trying to put the world to rights on her own. Much better to accept the world as it is, as inevitable." All the company looked at him in astonishment. He was talking common sense.

Dr. Robert, however, asked: "I thought that your book about the dilemma of victory was trying to find a solution to a problem. But per'aps I am wrong and do you an injustice."

"Don't stick your claws into me, Proust," said St. Clair, for the cat had leapt up to his shoulder.

"The dilemma of victory is a psychological, and not an economic, problem. Socialism is a mirage and economics hooey."

But Sir Samuel was more interested in what St. Clair might say about literature than in his social or political views. "What year was it when you saw so much of Proust? You must have been quite a young boy."

"Indeed I was," sighed St. Clair. "I was young but I was precocious." He nodded his head, ruminating, and it seemed as though he had no more to say. Then his eye brightened and he opened his mouth wide and said slowly:

"I was to Proust what Rimbaud was to Verlaine."

Complete silence greeted this remark. Then Pasionaria got up and left the room.

"Of course Proust's temperament could scarcely have been less like Verlaine's," St. Clair conceded. "And there was no Madame Proust to complicate our relationship. One cannot push the parallel too far as regards details. No, it was in thinking of myself as a young boy that the Rimbaud image came to me. We were very like indeed."

"*Tiens*," said Dr. Robert.

"But you diverged later," said Sir Sam gently.

"Oh yes." St. Clair paused again. "The first war was my flight from literature—comparable, if you insist, with Rimbaud's flight from literature and poetry to gun-running and Somaliland.

"But long before that, as I said earlier, I was able to put Proust on to a new and rewarding path in the

29

Recherche du Temps Perdu. It was as much accidental as deliberate. I don't claim any particular merit. It was purely that I was, I may say, the only one of Marcel's young boy friends who had read *The Golden Bowl* and had apprehended *The Lesson of the Master.*"

"Wonderfully convincing if one can get the dates to fit," said Sir Sam. "But why has no one published anything about it? I have never seen your friendship mentioned."

St. Clair waved a deprecating hand. "I have only myself to blame, if there is blame. I have these old-fashioned reticences. What I would tell my friends—for I conceal nothing—I would frankly dislike to see in print. In spite of all the enlightenment which has burst on us in these latter years, the old-fashioned prejudices exist. I do not share them. But perhaps I am still a little afraid of them. In any case, I would not like to see the name of De Beaumont sullied."

"That's quite absurd. But I do understand," said Sir Sam.

"It may be so. It is true that I returned Proust's feeling for me. I loved the poor sick man." St. Clair paused, and after a little went on: "That is one reason why I called my cat after him—though there was another more important reason, wasn't there, old boy?" he said, turning to address the sleeping animal on his shoulder.

"And what was that?" asked Sir Sam, laughing.

"When he was a kitten I wanted him to grow up a snobbish cat and not to mix with the common rooftop *minets.* And the plan has succeeded. He *is* a very snobbish cat and has recently become a mousing member of the Jockey Club."

Sir Sam crowed with pleasure. Then St. Clair repeated,

savoring each word: "I loved the poor sick man. . . .
But I was never what you might call a fairy."

Dr. Robert muttered something that nobody could
catch, and Amadeo said quietly: "No, you are not a fairy.
But you have lived all your life in fairyland."

St. Clair chuckled. "Yes. A palpable hit and truer than
you know, my young friend. I was young. I came to Paris.
I became a friend of Guillaume Apollinaire, of Cocteau,
of Diaghilev. It was like wandering on to the stage of
La Boutique Fantasque."

"And how is Lady Billy?" asked Leela, who had not
been listening. There was something in the question which
produced tension, and the smile on Dr. Robert's face
disappeared.

"Very fit, I believe," said Sir Sam. "She has been sailing
her boat, the *Constance,* and I'm on my way to join her
for a day or two at Nice. I broke the journey to see
Mathieu again and to hear Amadeo's latest ideas."

"Are you interested in building a city on the moon,
sir?" asked Rollo. Sir Sam looked up and laughed. "Good
lord no. *Je m'en fous de la lune.* But Amadeo's ideas
depend on the programing of computers, and so we have
lots of things to talk about. I do my best to understand
what he tells me."

The visitors left soon afterward. As Alamein helped her
uncle into his coat, she said: "Can I come and talk to
you tomorrow?"

The doctor reflected.

"I am free after lunch until four o'clock."

"Expect me at two." She stood watching them, then
shut the door.

"Is Sir Samuel an old friend of yours?" asked Rollo
as they sat round before saying good night.

31

"We scarcely know him. But he is a great friend of Uncle Mathieu," said Pasionaria. "It's a strange story. He was a British agent in France during the war and was captured and tortured by the Germans. But one of the French jailers rescued him, more dead than alive, and he was taken to our uncle by the Resistance. *La tante* Fidèle was a Pétainiste, of course, but she did not guess that the man she was nursing was an Englishman and a British agent. In the end he told her, but she had become attached to him."

"She knew what the Germans had done to him. It was unspeakable. We believed that he would never be able to marry," said Leela eagerly.

Alamein made a face and left the room, slamming the door.

"What is the matter with that girl?" asked Leela. Nobody replied. "But then, as I was going to say, he married the Lady Billy Flint. Very smart. Very English, very out of door. But what kind of marriage, I ask myself. What do they *do* together?"

"That's enough of that, Leela," said St. Clair unexpectedly.

Leela flushed and sat straight up in her chair, reproved.

"What do you say, Kitson, to his making millions of chaps unemployed?" St. Clair asked solemnly.

"Trades unions will have something to say about that," ventured Rollo.

"England would be a damned sight better off without the working classes," said St. Clair. "I always thought so, and now with this automation it is coming true. I may go back and live there if they are all got rid of."

In the doctor's house Amadeo and Sir Samuel sat up talking to their host after Yseult had gone to bed.

"Would you like a cup of chocolate?"

Sir Sam shook his head.

"I make myself a cup. It is good to sleep on."

"I would rather have whisky, if you have got it."

When Dr. Robert had settled down Sir Sam asked:

"Tell me about St. Clair de Beaumont."

"You must never believe a word he says," said the doctor.

"Nobody does," added Amadeo.

"Yet there must be something behind it all. There are, after all, the books," urged Sir Sam.

"There are two opinions about the books," said Amadeo.

"I suppose he really did know Proust," said Sir Sam.

Dr. Robert shrugged his shoulders. "It is quite possible he may have met him. But he certainly did not know him intimately."

"The one about Rimbaud was new to me," said Amadeo.

"Yes. I could see him invent it. He always opens his mouth very wide before bringing out a new invention. I have watched him doing it dozens of times," said Dr. Robert.

"But what is the truth?" asked Sir Sam.

"Surely you know that truth is relative. If St. Clair goes on saying that he was Rimbaud to Proust's Verlaine, it will become one of the truths which critics discover in literary textbooks," said Amadeo. Dr. Robert sipped his cocoa and said:

"St. Clair is, or more likely was, a brave man. He enlisted in the French army when he was only a boy and won the Croix de Guerre in the first war and the British George Cross in the second. As you saw tonight, he is decorated with the Legion of Honor. Not for literature—not for telling lies and fairy tales about being Proust's catamite—but because of what he did during the liberation."

"So he might have told the General to grow a forelock," said Sir Sam, laughing.

"We are all quite sure he didn't."

"He must know that. And that being so, can you explain his pouring out what you all know are lies?" asked Sir Sam.

"Well, St. Clair was always fond of telling tall stories, even before the war, when he married my sister. But the habit has grown enormously, and I think that it may be because he helped to operate a secret wireless station during the second war. It was supposed to be in France. He devoted a great deal of his time to inventing and denouncing scandals among the members of the Vichy Government. I was too busy with my patients to listen much."

"You were too busy organizing the Resistance," interrupted Sir Sam.

"Yes, that kept me busy too. But many of my patients listened to St. Clair. He came on the air for about half an hour every day, and in almost every talk there was some new dirt about the men of Vichy. Most people who listened believed every word of it, and almost all of it was true in spirit. I mean, if the details were wrong, they might so easily have been correct. Many of the things that St. Clair invented are now part of the history of France during the Occupation. They are accepted as true. And the extraordinary thing is that so many of the things were so nearly true that it seems hardly worth while to correct them in order to replace them with a version which is only a tedious variation on his inventions."

"But I suppose a lot of what he said *was* true," said Sir Sam.

"Yes. He was supplied with very good intelligence. And then of course he talked about the Germans. He was marvelous at inventing scandals among them which shortly afterward turned out to be true. Then he had higher flights of the imagination and invented conspiracies about subjects which have only begun to worry people twenty years later," said Dr. Robert.

"Yes, he invented a conspiracy of the Technocrats," said Amadeo.

"Exactly. Well now that he hasn't got the opportunity to let his imagination run riot for half an hour every day, St. Clair is rather bored. He writes books, but he writes too many. So on social occasions he relaxes and indulges his gift, which meets with little appreciation from his daughters. They suffer," said Dr. Robert.

"They think that he is a clown," said Amadeo. "And of course they are quite right. I tell them that a lot of the world's great men have been clowns—Picasso, for example, is a clown and proud of it—and I tell them it is the greatest mistake to be ashamed of one's parents."

"Yes, but one that can't be avoided. And it would take a girl with a strong stomach not to be ashamed of St. Clair at times."

"And what did you think of Winston's financier friend?" asked Amadeo, turning to Sir Sam.

"Mr. Kitson?" Sir Sam asked in a tone of surprise, as though it were strange that anybody should give him a thought. "He's not a financier. I thought for a moment that he was a confidence trickster. But he hasn't the imagination. He's a salesman."

Alamein tapped on the window of the office, and her uncle came and opened the door.

"Well what is it now, my little tart? You aren't pregnant,

are you?" The remark had the result that he expected: Alamein blushed, and when she blushed she was very pretty. But he paid for it by forfeiting the kiss with which she always greeted him.

"Don't be so obvious," she said angrily. "You think that all one's worries are physical."

"So it is mental, is it?" And he drew her toward him, and in spite of her reluctance kissed her tenderly on the cheek. She sat down and said: "You see, this Englishman coming here started me thinking. Pash is wildly attracted by him. But she says she would never have a love affair with any man before getting married. But in any case he's not attracted. At first I was very shocked at her wanting to marry a man she knows nothing about. But I see now that I might do the same. In fact, I probably shall."

Dr. Robert said nothing, but looked at her serious young face wrinkled in thought.

"Why does one believe one thing and secretly one is driven to do the opposite? It disgusts me to think that I am one person at one moment and another an hour later. I want to be consistent and not a mass of contradictions. There must be one standard of behavior that one can stick to."

"I don't think that there is in sexual matters," said her uncle. "People always pretend that there is, but it is a pretense."

"Well explain what you mean, because I don't understand why you think sexual matters are different from anything else," said Alamein, looking at him rather fiercely.

"You said just now that you were one person at one moment and another person a few minutes later. Well that is actually true. You are two people who have conflicting desires."

"What do you mean? How can I be?"

"Every kind of animal and plant, with the possible exception of bacteria, consists of two forms of existence which alternate. One form of the species has X number of chromosomes in all its cells, the other form having twice the number—2X. In some plants—the ferns—the two forms are completely separate and look like different plants. The fern, you know, produces spores each of which has half the number of chromosomes of the fern itself. The spore germinates and grows into a green little plant like a plate which later on produces eggs and spermatozoa. The nucleus of the spermatozoon penetrates into an egg, and the fertilized egg with the 2X number of chromosomes grows into a fern."

"What has all that got to do with me and what I am asking you?" interrupted Alamein.

"Listen and you may understand. . . . But in most plants and in all animals the cells which produce the eggs or the spermatozoa live like parasites contained in the body with the 2X number of chromosomes. So the existence of the 1X generation is hidden and is not suspected. That is the case with you and me. But each set of cells makes demands which are often contradictory in their nature. Samuel Butler, who was a shrewd thinker, though not a scientist, said that reproduction took place not because the parents wanted to reproduce, but because of the discontent of the germs with their surroundings inside the parents and a desire for separate existence. I think that he was right. So was Sterne when he wrote about the troubles of the poor little homunculus in *Tristram Shandy*. What you are complaining of is that the

37

demands of the eggs in your ovaries clash with your ordinary day-to-day life and the standards of your ordinary asexual behavior. In other words, the demands of the eggs in women and of the spermatozoa in men drive them to acts which surprise them. The poor little things have only twenty-three chromosomes instead of forty-six; they have no intelligence and probably no senses except that of touch and that of taste or smell, and they are easily tricked. Man spends a good deal of time in inventing ways of tricking them. Nevertheless their demands are exceedingly powerful, and they do impose a double standard of behavior on all of us. And it is no good pretending that we can avoid that, or fuse the two standards into one. I do not believe that they can be reconciled. The rationalists are always trying to do that, but their attempts usually turn out to be ludicrous. Somewhere or other they draw the line. On the other hand the churches admit that there are two standards, which they call God's and the Devil's. They would like us to be ferns, with no sexual lives. But we are not, and that is our glory. Our flowers are not only the sexual act itself and things directly concerned with it, such as brothels, but music, poetry, painting, ballet, and art of every kind."

"But why not acknowledge our sexual desires frankly? Why have two standards?"

"Because they are not the desires of our ordinary selves. They are the desires of the concealed creatures inside us and they express them in demands which we often feel are outrageous even in ourselves and disgust us in other people. What is necessary to the spermatozoon, or to the egg, horrifies the consciousness of the somatic cells."

"Are you telling me that I was once an egg forcing my parents to beget me against their will?"

"No. You were never an egg. There was an egg and a lucky spermatozoon, and when their nuclei fused you came suddenly into existence, an entirely new individual with all your curious physical and mental characteristics different from every human being that has ever existed. You cannot be traced back before that fusion. And you have no responsibility for the demands which that egg made of your mother or that the spermatozoon made of your father. And you are not responsible for the demands of the eggs in your ovaries."

"You have invented all this in order to put the blame for sin on a poor little homunculus that can't answer back," said Alamein, laughing.

"I am a scientist and I do not believe in sin. But I am telling you that there are two standards of value, or of behavior. Each of them is equally necessary. Because they conflict we conceal most of our sexual lives and usually hide part of them even from our sexual partners. I have had to, and I expect that you will have to do the same."

"Oh to be a fern with lovely curly fronds, cool and with only one standard of behavior," said Alamein, stretching out her arms.

"To be sure, the demands of the hidden 1X cells apart, one standard of behavior is essential for honest people. All the same, it is rare. The great majority of men have a different code of ethics for business. I agree that a double standard of behavior about money or personal advantage is profoundly immoral. It is almost universal in politics, where it results in injustice and cruelty. But a double standard about sex is inevitable because the demands of the sex cells are irreconcilable with decent behavior. And just as their existence as a separate form of human life is scarcely recognized, so their demands are unrecognized and misapprehended."

39

"I understand but I don't know whether you are right," said Alamein.

"Well now, my hart's-tongue fern, give me a kiss. And as all this is leading up to your seducing that dull Englishman, you must know how to play tricks. Otherwise I shall have you getting pregnant or catching venereal disease, and to prevent that is what I am here for."

3

Rollo lay awake that night turning things over in his mind and felt sure that he was really on to a big thing— a very big thing. He considered sleepily what they should call it. The parent company had better be: Telefaction Ltd. Then there might be two subsidiaries: Automatic Armies and First City in the Moon, Inc. Neither sounded quite right. Perhaps First Lunar City and Automation Armaments. And then, since he himself was going to be chairman of the group of companies, his name ought to appear. Perhaps the first city in the moon should be called Kitson. That would be far better than Lunaville, which merely suggested an asylum. The word lunar, with its association of lunatics and lunacy, had better be kept out of the prospectus altogether.

In fact, the more emphasis they put on telefaction the better. It was a magnificent word, and he had better see about taking out world rights in it as a trade-mark. Or was the word "Telefactors" better? Yes, it was. Quite definitely, Telefactors was the right name for the group.

If he could get the old Yid De Beaumont to put up £10,000, it would cover promotion expenses nicely. Alamein would help in that. In fact, Alamein was probably the key to the whole thing. Suppose he married Alamein? He would be in a very strong position as regards Amadeo Severin. Anyway, she was a damned attractive kid. But of course whatever cash old De Beaumont and anyone else he could string along—such as Mrs. Lorriner—could put up would only be chicken feed. The thing was to get the public wild about getting in on the ground floor—and then hanging on until he could get people like Vickers or Rolls-Royce interested. And settling himself comfortably in bed, Rollo played first with the thought of Alamein and then with the possibility of a seat on the board of Rolls-Royce or English Electric, or whatever big fish would be ready to open its mouth and swallow them. He was asleep.

The following day was devoted to second thoughts. Doubts assailed both the inventor and his financier—and Winston and his sisters were kept busy in allaying them.

Amadeo Severin wanted to know something definite about Captain Kitson's credentials as a financier. What was his standing in the City of London? With which of the great banking houses was he associated? Was his father on the board of one of the internationally famous companies such as Shell?

So, shortly after breakfast, Amadeo appeared at the Château de Berri with an unusually bleak expression and carried off Winston into the park to the old fourteenth-century dovehouse, where he could grill him undisturbed.

Rollo Kitson, on his part, woke up feeling entirely skeptical about the very notion of telefaction and had no doubts whatever that the first city in the moon, which he had so optimistically named Kitson the previous night, was so much moonshine.

Of course he was clear enough in his mind to realize that it did not really matter a damn whether telefaction was, or was not, under any circumstances a physical possibility. All that mattered was that investors should be tumbling over each other to get in on the ground floor.

On the other hand it did matter quite a lot. Because if Amadeo had invented nothing but the word "telefaction" and was merely destined for the loony bin, there was obviously no sense in giving him a large share in the company. Yet if he could strike matches, not, perhaps, on the moon, but at the other end of a cricket pitch, he would have a distinct value. And of course it was essential to take him in, at any rate for a bit, in order to get the old Yid De Beaumont to cough up 10,000 smackers. And Alamein was completely sold on her cousin's genius.

Altogether it looked as though he had better tread warily and go slow. If Amadeo could produce nothing tangible, it would be just possible to go it alone and try to sell the notion for what it was worth. That is what he would have to do if he could only touch his host for fifty quid.

On the other hand it would be very difficult to play it alone. It was pretty well essential to have a back-room boy up one's sleeve. And in a moment of self-knowledge Rollo realized that it was psychologically essential for himself for there to be a "back-room boy" even if he didn't believe that he was a genius who could perform what he claimed. Without someone of the kind he would feel naked; like Hans Andersen's Emperor in his birthday suit.

Probably he couldn't "go it alone," and Amadeo would be necessary. But it would be difficult to get any definite facts out of Alamein. Perhaps Pash had a more cynical head on her shoulders; so Rollo sought her out after breakfast.

Pasionaria seemed quite ready to meet his wishes half-way and led him off to a little gazebo looking out over the moat which ran behind the château, though it had been filled in on the front side and replaced by the ha-ha.

43

Rollo filled his pipe and took some time getting to his subject.

"It has been quite wonderful coming here and dropping in to such a rich and rewarding—isn't that how Henry James would describe you all?—cluster of human beings. I suppose what I'm asking is a bit—well, intimate—but I wish you'd tell me something about Leela. For me she is the mystery woman."

"What is mysterious about her?"

"Well, what is her background? I don't think she is French, is she? And she certainly isn't English."

"She is a White Russian, born and brought up in Paris, who married an English country solicitor. But she found life intolerable in Gloucestershire and left him. She met my parents in London during the war when they were refugees. My mother was working in the French section of the B.B.C. and so was Leela. She became one of my mother's greatest friends and my father's mistress and came back here with my father and mother after the war was over—in 1946. My mother died two years later, in 1948, when I was ten."

"Tell me about your mother and her family."

"Mother was an intensely active and absolutely unpractical idealist. She spent nine-tenths of her life in sitting on committees. Originally it was the Union of Democratic Control—long before I was born. Then it was the League of Nations Union. Then it was anti-fascism and the Peace Ballot and all the committees for helping the Spanish loyalists during the Civil War. And of course opposing Hitler and opposing rearmament at the same time. Finally, after the betrayal of Czechoslovakia, came the Second World War."

"What did your father do in that?" asked Rollo.

"Oh, Father did a hush-hush job. I never believe what

44

he tells one about it. But he did make money by gambling on victory," said Pasionaria contemptuously. However, Rollo's face brightened.

"Meaning?" he asked.

"You know, there wasn't any gasoline, so no one bought expensive cars. Well, Father took up options on several hundred new, or nearly new cars, and sold them at a huge profit before the car manufacturers got back to building cars after the war, while there were still long waiting lists."

"So he was in England all through it? Oh, I remember Winston telling me that he and Alamein were both born in England during the war."

"No, he went back to France six months before D-day, as a link with the Resistance. Luckily my parents got to England before the fall of France. They would both have been sent to a concentration camp by the Nazis. Then of course my mother got the job in the French section of the B.B.C."

"What was she like as a person?" asked Rollo. It was a surprising question, because he was usually more interested in who people were than in what they were like, but it had occurred to him that perhaps Pash was the one who was most like her mother.

"What most people felt about her was that she was a terrific aristocrat. She had complete self-assurance. When she got an idea into her head, she could not be diverted. Unfortunately the causes she espoused were usually doomed to failure—the only exception was the last war to defeat Hitler and Mussolini."

"Must have been a terrifying old trout," said Rollo.

Pasionaria gazed at him speechless for a moment and then replied: "How dare you speak of my mother like that, you impertinent brute."

45

"Oh, sorry. Just a slip of the tongue," Rollo answered, and looked at the angry girl with a puzzled smile of surprise.

"It was an insult, and I think that you had better . . ." But Rollo interrupted with:

"I'm damned sorry. I didn't mean anything. I had no idea you would take it like that." And Rollo put his hands on Pasionaria's shoulders.

"Please, please forgive me. . . ." And he drew her to him and kissed the unresponsive mouth.

"You are just trying to make me forget what a rude, coarse soldier you are," said Pasionaria, yielding as he drew her down to sit beside him on the garden seat. He kissed her again. After another kiss she softened and returned his kiss, closing her eyes, and clutching his shoulders.

But no sooner had she softened and melted into his arms than Rollo began to disengage himself gently from her embrace.

"Please go on telling me about your mother. I really do want to know about her and about everything that has to do with you, Pash," he said humbly.

At this point Pasionaria would have much preferred to drop the subject; however, she went on:

"As I was saying, she was an aristocrat by birth as well as character. She was the only child of the Baron du Bartas, and her mother was a Bentinck—Dutch. She was also very handsome. I am supposed to be like her."

Pasionaria laughed, and at that moment, with her white teeth shining in her brown face, her dark eyes sparkling, and her glistening black tresses hanging round her little shell-like ears, she did look extremely handsome. Most men would have taken advantage of the opportunity offered, but Rollo was unresponsive. He liked to know where he was going and he was unprepared for embraces with consequences that might lead him away from his planned course of action.

A bit too red hot, this one, he thought to himself. Later on he was to phrase it: "Doesn't she just live up to her name!"

So he only nodded his head sagely, fingered his pipe, and after remarking that he had always heard from Winston that their mother was a fine woman, he changed the subject abruptly with the request: "Now tell me about your uncle and his nephew and that side of the family."

"You're very thorough, Captain Kitson," replied Pasionaria, thinking that he was a heavy uncouth fellow not to rise to pay the compliment which her words had demanded.

"Let me see, what can I tell you? My mother's step-father was General Robert of the Genie—the sappers. I really don't know much about him except that he resigned from the army at the time of the *Affaire* because he believed that Dreyfus was innocent. Also he had brains, and I think that it was from him that my mother imbibed her extreme radical populist views.

"General Robert had a daughter, Celeste, by an earlier marriage, who married a Venetian doctor and their son, Amadeo Severin, is the inventor. Our uncle believes that he is a very great genius whose name will rank with Curie and Marconi."

"How does he show it?"

"You had better ask to see one of his experiments."

"Have you ever seen one?"

Pasionaria nodded. "I did not see it—but I know about it. I don't know quite how secret it is, and you must be careful not to repeat what I say. But Amadeo once drove a car all the way here from Bonnefous—over sixteen kilo-

47

meters—while he was sitting in his laboratory. Alamein was in the driving seat and she did not touch the controls once all the way. She was there only in order that the experiment should not attract attention when their car passed other cars on the road."

"And she had the nerve to sit there doing nothing with other cars passing her?"

Pasionaria laughed. "But of course. She said she sometimes put her hands lightly on the steering wheel and that it was uncanny to feel it moving of its own accord under her fingers when they came to a bend in the road. But how funny you look, Captain Kitson." For Rollo was staring with a sort of dazed fascination.

"Of course Alamein is like a Trilby, with Amadeo as Svengali." But Rollo was not listening any more.

"So that's what he means when he talks about tele-faction," he said. "Well I'll see Alamein and get it direct from the horse's mouth," he muttered. Pasionaria had sold him the idea more completely than Amadeo with all his talk of automatic armies and a city on the moon.

"Thanks a lot. You've been wonderful, Pash. And we are pals, now, aren't we?" He got up and, leaving her to follow, hurried off in search of her sister.

If Pasionaria had sold Amadeo to Rollo, Winston had entirely failed with the reverse operation. His impassioned advocacy of his friend had, however, seemed so irrelevant and futile to Amadeo that none of the discredit had attached itself to Rollo—only to Winston. Obviously it was not Mr. Kitson's fault that Winston was a half-witted, sentimental, unconscious homosexual. Winston's idiocy proved nothing, and Amadeo was sufficiently clear-headed to dismiss the hour and a half which he had spent grilling him in the pigeon house as wasted. It occurred to him that Alamein, who was neither sentimental nor half-witted, might have picked up some information about the visitor.

But when he had returned with a surly Winston stalking silently beside him to the château, he found that Alamein was gone. Leela was glad to see him; she was in a state of some excitement. Half an hour earlier Captain Kitson had returned from a walk in the park with Pash and had immediately asked Alamein to go with him to Paris "for a jaunt."

Alamein had accepted with alacrity, had rushed upstairs and changed her clothes in an incredibly short space of time, while Captain Kitson was getting out his car, and they had driven off together. When Leela had realized what was happening she had called out: "What time will you be back?" And Alamein had answered: "Oh, expect us when you see us."

"Just think of their going off to Paris! And Captain Kitson never bothered to ask St. Clair's permission. St. Clair hates being interrupted when he is writing. Ought I to go and tell him, or shall I wait till lunch?"

Amadeo shrugged his shoulders, protruded his lower lip, and suddenly gave an unpleasant, disconcerting laugh. Leela felt that she might have known that he would be no help to her. And Amadeo realized that Rollo Kitson's taking off Alamein without family discussion, or even a mention of when they would return, though it annoyed him personally, prepossessed him in his favor. It was a sign of capacity for action, which was just what he wanted in a partner.

For the first time it seemed to him that Rollo Kitson might be the man who he had hoped would eventually turn up. And without asking himself when the pair would return from their joy ride, and having nothing left to do at the Château de Berri, Amadeo got on his bicycle and pedaled home.

Trembling with anger, Pasionaria knocked at her father's door and marched in without waiting. St. Clair was correcting proofs.

"I think you ought to know that Alamein and Captain Kitson have gone off to Paris together," she said woodenly.

"Much obliged for the news. But why is it you who tell me? Did she ask you to?"

"No she did not. And if I had guessed that she was going, I should have told her to ask your permission herself."

"As of course you would have done, my dear Pash, if Captain Kitson had invited you to be his companion on the jaunt."

"Knowing what I do about him, I should have refused. That is probably why he didn't ask me," said Pasionaria.

"If you would have refused the invitation, I can't see what you are worrying about," drawled her father.

"He is quite untrustworthy. He spent an hour trying to worm everything about our family and about Amadeo out of me. Then when I got angry he tried to make it up by kissing me, and when I wouldn't have that, he rushed off to try and find out more from Alamein. No doubt he thinks if he can get her alone and make love to her, she will tell him everything."

"I can't imagine what she ought not to tell him. But thank you, Pash. It was very loyal of you to come and tell me about it. Now I'll go on correcting my proofs," said St. Clair.

Speechless with anger at her father's use of the word "loyal," which she knew was sarcastic, Pasionaria went quietly out of the room.

———

"Well thank God we've escaped from them all," said Rollo, shifting his eyes for a moment from the road in front to the lovely cheek and fluttering tresses of the girl beside him.

"Escaped? Does that mean you don't like staying with us?" asked Alamein. She knew as she said it that she wasn't being quite sincere; she herself felt that she had escaped. It was natural and right and proper that she should, since she was one of the family. But a visitor, like Rollo, had no business to speak of "escaping" while enjoying their hospitality.

"I like being with *you*," said Rollo. "It's because I have wanted so much to be alone with you that I felt the only thing was to escape together to Paris and get away from Winston."

"Winston's one of your greatest friends, isn't he?"

"Rather. The dear old boy. But one gets a bit tired of him."

Alamein thought it might be a mistake to take this up, though the disloyalty of Rollo's words made her feel sorry.

"Do you know Paris well?" she asked after a silence.

Rollo's knowledge of Paris was sketchy and peculiar.

"All I know is the Eiffel Tower and the Place de la Concorde. I rely on you to be my guide to the town. Where are you going to take me?"

"Well, how much money can we spend?" asked Alamein.

Rollo laughed warmly, humorously, and with a curious content.

"No you don't," he said. "I can find my way to the Ritz by myself. What I want is for you to show me the sort of place students of your age go to. It's not a question of money. It's just that more than anything I want to know

51

about your life. You see, you and your life are very important to me, Alamein."

"I wasn't thinking of taking you to the Ritz. I only wondered if you had enough for a theater as well as a dinner."

"Yes, we could run to both." And Rollo began to ask her how well she knew Paris and how often she was able to escape from Leela and Pash and go about the city alone. And in everything he said there was a suggestion that all her family were rather comic and tiresome people and that he had been staying with them, and putting up with them, simply in the hope of getting to know her better.

Alamein felt sorry that Rollo should feel like that about them, but she was at the same time a good deal flattered. Because to be taken off by him at a moment's notice, to sit beside him in his little racing car with her hair blowing out straight behind her like an advertisement of a high-octane gasoline was simply marvelous. Rollo was big and muscular and masculine and he spoke with more authority than any man she had ever known—and he liked her particularly. He was marvelous, and the faint stirrings of criticism were lulled to sleep. After all, her family were very ordinary people compared with him.

"Let's stop at the next place and buy food and wine and have a picnic lunch. That will save money for Paris," suggested Alamein. She was thinking not of the francs saved but that it would be easier if they picnicked together in a wood to find out quite what Rollo's liking for her amounted to, and how far it would take him. Also, she preferred picnics to restaurants.

Rollo would have preferred lunch in a pleasant roadside restaurant with a table and comfortable chairs, a good helping of *poulet de Bresse,* and an attentive waiter. However, he fell in with Alamein's suggestion saying:

52

"You buy whatever you prefer. You're the expert and I'm in your hands."

They stopped in the next little town, and while Rollo had the tank filled with gasoline and the tires checked, Alamein bought bread, butter, *terrine de lièvre, crème fraîche,* and strawberries, with a bottle of *Blanc des Blancs* from the Marne. A few miles farther on they stopped at a spot where the forest ended on a slope above a stretch of water. While they were carrying cushions and parcels from the car, Alamein caught Rollo's eye, and when they had put them down they looked at each other again and a moment later he was giving her a thoughtful kiss. Her young, muscular, yielding body and her almost incredibly soft lips excited him more than he had expected, but he was the one who brought the embrace to an end. He was aware that if he let himself go, he might easily bring about a reaction in a young virgin. So he discreetly introduced a new subject.

"You know, my pet, I'm very much excited about the prospects of Amadeo's inventions. They are awfully interesting, and I think it's extraordinarily lucky that I've come along just at this time. Because I feel sure that with the faith I have in him, I can make a great success of this revolutionary idea. He needs me, or someone like me, and I feel that, if he only agrees, we can work wonderfully together."

Alamein had looked slightly sulky because he had released her too soon from his embrace, but now her eyes brightened.

"Yes, I can see it's true. It might possibly be a wonderful combination. Amadeo and you are the two men I know who are most unlike. So you might be complementary. He is all brain and intelligence; you are *savoir-*

vivre." Discerning a faint cloud on her companion's face she went on:

"Amadeo's intelligence is purely abstract, but you understand people, only perhaps you are sometimes too critical of them."

"I wouldn't be able to define the difference in words," said Rollo. "But directly I met him I felt we might make a good team, filling up each other's deficiencies, and that we could, if we worked together, make a good thing of telefaction."

"I know you could—if only you and Amadeo could work together. It wouldn't be easy. But I suppose if you feel you can, you will be able to."

"I am pretty sure we can. You see, I don't mind his being an egotist."

"An egotist? I should never have thought of calling Amadeo one. Perhaps he is, in a way," said Alamein.

"Surely you can see that, my pet?" And Rollo laughed and, taking her by the hand, drew her to him.

"There are such a lot of things I don't see. The fact is I'm a fearful fool," Alamein said to herself while she was being kissed, and when Rollo released her almost immediately and exclaimed in a businesslike way: "And now for Paris!" she replied: "I know I'm a fool. I'm very blind."

"You!" cried Rollo, with a catch of his breath. "You are the most wonderful girl I have ever met. You have real intuition and understanding and sympathy. I think you are just miraculous."

"Don't make fun of me," said Alamein, and there were tears trembling in her eyes, only Rollo did not notice because he had started the car and was backing it out of the wood onto the road.

"I would never dream of making fun of you. I love you

too much," he said soberly as they set off on the road to Paris. He felt shaken by an unusual emotion. He realized that he did love the kid: he did think that she was bloody marvelous, and there was nothing he wouldn't do to make her happy.

Alamein choked back her momentary impulse to weep and realized that what he was saying was true. He did love her too much to make fun of her, and in that he was the exact opposite of Amadeo, who never stopped making fun of her, because that was his way of showing his love.

In Paris they ate and drank and watched a floor show and then danced and drank champagne and finally drove back to the Château de Berri in the early hours of the morning. But although they kissed several times they did not talk any more about Amadeo and telefaction. The door of the château was unlocked, but there was no one sitting up: only a message from Leela to say:

"Soup in the oven."

They each drank a cupful and then, after a last passionate kiss from Alamein, tiptoed quietly up the stairs to their separate rooms.

Yes, Rollo was in love with Alamein and as he got into bed with the savor of her last kisses (somewhat overlaid by toothpaste) on his lips, he recognized the fact and the danger of upsetting all his plans if their love became known too soon. He felt sure that Amadeo was more than a little in love with his pretty young cousin. So first Alamein must sell him the idea that he, Rollo, was the heaven-sent businessman and financial genius who could float Telefaction. Then he must make a cast-iron agreement with Amadeo, and only after that was signed and sealed and witnessed in front of the proper kind of *notaire public* or *huissier* would it be wise to announce his engagement to Alamein and then immediately to get the "old Yid" to put up £10,000 for the Telefaction flotation.

Yes, that was the logical order of the moves required during the coming week or so. He had been a good deal tempted to let himself go with Alamein—but that would never have done. Amadeo must sign on the dotted line first, before he heard any rumor of love, engagement, or marriage. And then, when the agreement was out of the way, the news of the engagement breaking before any financial talks would put him in a pretty strong position in dealing with old De Beaumont. It was wonderful how well things often worked out if you took them one at a time and in the right order. He fell asleep cozily content.

Not so Alamein. She felt far too furious with herself to fall asleep. She knew that any other girl in the world would have done better. Rollo had actually said that he loved her, and she felt almost sure that he was telling the truth when he said it. But he hadn't spoken of making love and had three times broken off his thrilling kisses and had never hinted at anything more. Probably he thought she was only a child and felt he ought to "respect her" because of her youth. She would just show him.

Anyway it was a glorious idea that he should help Amadeo to get his inventions taken up. She would talk to Amadeo next morning and make him understand what a marvelous chance it was for him. Not that she herself was disinterested about it. Though she couldn't explain all that to Amadeo. Because if Rollo didn't become Amadeo's partner, he would just drive off to the South of France and ten to one he would be lost to them forever. In spite of his kisses she would never see him again. Whereas if he was busy helping Amadeo he would quite likely stay on with them, and—who knows—it might end in his making a success of the invention and marrying her.

If he wanted to, she would go to the moon with him. The danger was that he was so critical of people. He wanted to escape from them. He found Winston's devotion to him a bore, Amadeo an egotist, her father a comic figure. . . . Heaven knows what he really thought of Leela and even of so experienced a person as Pash. How could she hope to hold anyone who had such impossibly high standards?

And Alamein clenched her fists and her naked toes and clamped her jaws. Thank God he was interested in Telefaction and anxious to help Amadeo. That was the way to hold him.

"I know nothing about this financial friend of Winston's," repeated St. Clair for the third time, glaring across the breakfast table at Leela and Pasionaria. "I am left in total ignorance. I neither approve of his running off with Alamein to Paris for the entire evening and most of the subsequent night, nor do I disapprove. I was not consulted; I have not been informed. But you tell me that they have at least returned to shelter under my roof."

"They each drank a cupful of soup when they got back," said Leela soothingly.

"That tells me nothing. The greatest rascal unhung will drink soup. So may a perfectly decent fellow," conceded St. Clair.

"Why go on talking about it, if you don't know any of the facts?" asked Pasionaria.

"I want to *constater le fait*. All I say is that I know nothing about this financier. I have been left in the dark. No doubt I am to blame. For all I know, the fellow may come of decent and honorable people. Any blot on the scutcheon may be forgiven if it occurred centuries ago."

"What in hell are you talking about, St. Clair?" asked

Pasionaria in a genuinely puzzled tone. "What blot on what scutcheon?"

"I ask myself what is Kitson? The most likely answer is that the name arises from Kitty's son: Kitty's bastard. He might have you as his father, mightn't he, you old rascal," he said addressing the cat on his shoulder and turning his head, so that Proust could rub his head against his cheek. "But it might be, almost equally well, Christopher's son—and a perfectly legitimate son at that. I don't know. I am in the dark. I suspend judgement."

At this moment Winston came into the room and helped himself to bacon and egg and tomato from the hot plate and then waited while his father filled him a bowl of coffee.

"I daresay Winston can tell us something, at all events," said Leela.

"Our father is complaining that he knows nothing about Captain Kitson, who may be the greatest rascal in the world although he drinks soup," said Pasionaria in her usual contemptuous tone of voice.

"What on earth do you mean by calling Rollo a rascal?" asked Winston, already furious.

"Captain Kitson and Alamein didn't return from Paris until four o'clock in the morning, and your father is naturally worried," said Leela.

St. Clair shrugged his shoulders and brushed up his mustaches. "I never said I was worried. All I say is that he may be an honorable man, or he may not. I don't know."

"I can answer that," cried Winston furiously. "Rollo is the bravest of the brave. He risked his life during a riot in Famagusta trying to save the life of a little Turkish boy who had been knocked down by one of our armored cars. He was heartbroken when the boy died later in the hospital."

"My God. What did I tell you? I must have second sight!" exclaimed Pasionaria, but no one listened to her.

"Would you trust him with your sister's honor?" asked St. Clair portentously.

"I tell you I saw him push open the hatch, climb out, and pick the little fellow out of the gutter. And all the time he was doing it we were sitting targets for the chaps who had been lobbing grenades at us farther down the street."

"That was splendid. Courage is so beautiful, don't you agree with me, Pash?" cried Leela. "A woman feels it. A woman knows that it takes a man with buncombes to do a thing like that."

"What on earth are you trying to say, Leela?" asked St. Clair.

"With buncombes, as the Victorians said; with cajones, as Hemingway writes. With balls." Leela brought the words out defiantly and almost with pride.

At that moment the door opened and the hero with buncombes walked into the breakfast room.

His arrival was the signal for a sudden exit: Pasionaria left hurriedly because she was furious with Rollo for taking Alamein to Paris, Winston because he was afraid that his father would insult their guest, and St. Clair followed a moment or two later after a brief "Good morning."

"Aha! *The Times*," exclaimed Rollo, taking possession of it, and, producing a pencil, he turned to the crossword on the back page, only looking up for a moment at intervals to take a mouthful of eggs and bacon, or a pull at the bowl of coffee which Leela had set before him. She would have spoken, she would indeed dearly have liked to tell him that she felt deeply sympathetic about the little Turkish boy, only she was rather scandalized. To appropriate *The Times* was something which was never done, but which was perhaps just pardonable in a guest. But to do the crossword puzzle was to inflict a wound the smart of which would be felt by St. Clair for the following twenty-four hours.

What was to make it particularly galling was that Rollo did the crossword with such extreme rapidity that he had filled up the last light and pushed the paper aside within ten minutes, so that when St. Clair returned from the lavatory to reclaim the newspaper which he had accidentally left behind him, he saw the crossword lying uppermost completely filled in. It was a proof, if one were needed, that Rollo was a better man than he, or at any rate more astutely puzzle-minded. St. Clair usually spent an hour or two over it and never completed it at all. Rollo's feat was incredible, and by the time that St. Clair had reached his study it dawned on him that he must be the victim of a practical joke. Rollo must have bought a copy of that *Times* in Paris, where it could be got on the day of issue, have done the crossword at leisure, perhaps during the watches of the night, and then have copied the solution into St. Clair's copy when he found it lying on the breakfast table.

Directly he had thought of this explanation of a dastardly trick, St. Clair ran upstairs and dashed into Alamein's bedroom without even knocking.

His daughter looked up dewy-eyed with sleep and so radiantly lovely that any parent not obsessed by puzzles would have guessed that she was in love.

"When you and Captain Kitson were in Paris, did he . . ."

"I absolutely refuse to allow you to burst into my bedroom and make scenes. I am grown up. I shall leave here

60

this morning," cried Alamein, sitting upright in bed. She was scarlet with anger.

"Tell me the truth," thundered St. Clair. "Did he buy a copy of *The Times* in Paris?"

"Certainly not . . . Did he do what?"

"Did he buy a copy of *The Times?*"

"What has that got to do with anything?"

"He must have bought a copy. Otherwise he has done the crossword in about five minutes." And St. Clair explained how he had left *The Times* in the breakfast room and had returned in no more than ten minutes to find the crossword completed.

"No, he certainly did not buy a newspaper of any description. I must have seen it if he had," replied Alamein. She had recovered from her sudden fury, and looked at her father with an odd light in her eyes, feeling a mixture of affection, contempt, irritation, and amusement.

"Do you know, Daddy, that you are the most peculiar father for a young girl that could be found in the whole of France?" she asked him. Usually she called her father "St. Clair." "Daddy" was reserved for moments of intimacy.

"Am I? Oh, I meant to ask you: have you fallen in love with the fellow? Did he try and make love to you? Is there anything between you that you ought to tell me?"

"Get out of my bedroom. Buzz off. Don't dare ask me any more idiotic questions," Alamein howled at him. But her anger and indignation were pretended. Her father retired aware that he had put himself in a bad light by asking first about *The Times*. And he went back to his study to look at it. Could Rollo possibly be right in thinking that "dog Latin" was the correct solution for "a classic bay," he wondered. Surely the reference must be to a bay horse that had won the Derby, or one of the classic races? And then suddenly the reason for Rollo's solution dawned: dogs bay the moon. And that fellow had done the whole damned crossword in not more than ten minutes.

"I suppose it comes of his being a financial genius," St. Clair reflected sadly as he turned to the fourth leader.

After she had had breakfast, Alamein got on her bicycle and went off to the doctor's house, and Rollo, taking possession of St. Clair's study, and borrowing some sheets of note paper, began to draw up the terms on which he hoped to become Amadeo's associate.

TELEFACTORS: Capital £100,000 divided into 400,000 ordinary 5/- shares

Chairman and Managing Director: Captain Rollo Kitson

Director of Development and Research: M. Amadeo Severin

M. Severin has sold his patents to the company and has signed a contract giving his exclusive services to Telefactors Ltd. for a period of 20 years for the sum of £20,000 payable in the form of 80,000 fully paid-up ordinary shares. Captain Kitson has been allotted 40,000 fully paid ordinary shares on signing a service agreement with the company giving it his exclusive service for ten years.

The parent company, which will be registered in Geneva, exists to carry out constant research and to finance and control subsidiaries formed to undertake special projects which will be registered in New York, London, etc. as seems advisable.

The first two subsidiaries are likely to be

  (1) Automatic Armies,
  (2) First City of the Moon.

The Chairman will draw a salary of £3,000 per annum plus expenses and directors fees. He will work full time and his constant endeavor will be to secure powerful financial backing for Telefactors S.A. with bankers such as Lazard and Morgan and with great engineering firms such as Rolls-Royce in England and the General Electric Company of America.

Again and again Rollo scratched out one word and substituted another, again and again he deleted one row of figures and inserted another. Finally he was satisfied, and, inserting a sheet of paper in St. Clair's ancient typewriter, he laboriously typed out his proposals with two fingers and a thumb.

Meanwhile Alamein and Amadeo had taken refuge at the bottom of their uncle's vegetable garden behind a row of climbing haricots. Alamein was sitting on the ground, and her cousin was balanced on the handles of the wheelbarrow. Her arrival had been a surprise, because the De Beaumonts practically never risked meeting their aunt Fidèle. Fortunately, however, that lady was still in the meat market buying a tenderloin of pork for the evening meal. But as surprising as her arrival were the shining eyes and the light blush with which Alamein announced:

"I've come to talk to you about your business—about your inventions and about Rollo—Captain Kitson."

It seemed to Amadeo that in those words what she was really saying was:

"I've come to you at once to tell you that I have fallen in love with this English visitor at the château" and indeed had she put her message in those words, the pang that shot through him could have been no greater, nor could the feeling of tenderness, which made her happiness at that moment of paramount importance to him. Nothing he said or did must reveal the deadening shock of her message. At all costs those eyes must be left lustrous and that soft cheek glowing with the wonderful thing which had happened to her. And she was much too young to get married.

That Alamein did not speak of love but of company promotions, that she did not announce her own marriage, but pressed on him a lifelong partnership with Captain Kitson made no difference. Amadeo watched her with a gentle smile and at intervals repeated: "But of course . . . naturally . . . what could be more suitable?"

It had not occurred to him that by his words he was making Alamein's marriage more certain and that the way in which he could have got the better of his rival in love was to refuse to have any business dealings with him. He could not for a moment have imagined that love and business were linked, for he could read Alamein's love for Rollo in her eyes and in the tones of her voice when she spoke his name, and he concluded that all was settled between them. But even if Amadeo had suspected the truth, he would still have murmured acquiescence and agreement. For at that moment he could not have brought himself to have hurt Alamein. He could not have brought a look of astonishment, alarm, and grief into those shining eyes.

"Well it's all too wonderful. I'll tell Rollo that you agree to the partnership and that you will come round and see him this afternoon. He'll be wildly excited. And he'll be surprised that I'm such a good businesswoman. I suspect you are surprised too."

"No, I'm not. I have the highest admiration for your character and your intelligence," said Amadeo, and then added: "But in any case you know that I can refuse you nothing, even if I wanted to."

64

"But you don't want to, do you?"

"Good heavens no. I'm immensely grateful to you, darling." It was a relief to be able to have called her *"chérie"* and to have told her that he could refuse her nothing and it was a delight when she put her hand on his shoulder after she had risen to her feet and said:

"You are always so charming to me. I think I respect you more than anybody I know—and I love you a lot." With that she walked away gaily down the garden path and out of the side gate into the street. Amadeo followed her slowly and, as she mounted her bicycle, he was startled by his aunt's voice asking:

"What did she come for? What's going on?"

"She came to invite me to visit the château this afternoon," replied Amadeo, who knew from experience that his aunt's question had to be answered. Nevertheless he only shrugged his shoulders as she demanded: "Why didn't you bring her into the house?" By that time Alamein had reached the end of the street and was turning the corner. The street was empty, and Amadeo went back to his study.

If I am committed to partnership with this Englishman, I had much better plunge in and show all possible good will. And even if the association isn't quite what I was looking for, I expect that I am making it easier for Alamein to marry the man she is in love with, he reflected. All that matters is her happiness.

"Well done!" exclaimed Rollo after Alamein had returned and reported the result of her mission. "That's a fine girl! And do you think he's likely to be difficult?"

She stared at him blankly. "I don't know what you mean. I have just told you that he has agreed to take you as his partner."

"I mean difficult about terms. There are agreements to

be signed and that sort of thing. Will he drive a hard bargain?"

"He'll agree to anything that's fair, of course," said Alamein, using an exasperating word which all business-men know is meaningless. "You don't suppose that Amadeo would ever haggle about anything for his own advantage, do you?"

"Well, that's all I wanted to know. That is just splendid, darling," said Rollo, but he did not put out his hand to take hers and draw her to him.

"I'll just make fair copies of my drafts," he said. Alamein's eyes shone a little less happily and her brow was clouded as she went out of the room.

Amadeo proved as easy to deal with as she had foretold. After he had read through Rollo's draft, he asked why the period of the service agreement was twenty years in his case and only five in that of Rollo.

"Well, frankly, it's because you are absolutely indispensable to the business whereas the company may one day wish to get rid of me. In that case, if I had a long-term service agreement, I could claim a very large sum for loss of office," explained Rollo.

Secondly Amadeo wanted to know what his salary would be. No figure had been put down. Rollo had been expecting this question.

"Any figure is provisional. It depends on where one lives and so on. Shall I put your salary down provisionally at £2,000 a year?"

"I should think I could manage on that easily. But you see you'll also have to provide about four million pounds as soon as we can possibly borrow it for my laboratory equipment."

Rollo took this statement, which was unexpected, without blinking an eye.

"Yes, to be sure we will. But that is part of financing future research, I take it."

"All right then. So long as that's understood. But I would also suggest that we give Alamein a block of shares and that we put her on the board of directors," said Amadeo.

This suggestion was less generous than it sounded and more Machiavellian, and in making it Amadeo Severin felt he was taking out an insurance for the future. Whatever happened he could trust Alamein.

Rollo was surprised, but he welcomed the idea with a show of enthusiasm.

"What do you suggest? Something nominal? Shall we give her 500 shares?"

"I think 10,000 would be more reasonable. We owe her something."

"All right. Let's make it 10,000," said Rollo good-temperedly. "I'll get all the documents drawn up, and we can sign them in front of the *huissier* before I leave for the Midi."

That evening, after supper, he proposed to Alamein, and she threw herself joyfully into his arms. For the sake of privacy they had repaired to a large and little-used room called the Billiard Room because it had once held a billiard table some twenty years before. Indeed, there were still markers which could be slid to and fro along the wall. The table itself, with cues and balls, had been removed by the German invaders in 1941 to equip their officers' mess in the neighboring château at Rivenchy, and after the war the owners of that house had refused to return what they apparently regarded as spoils of war, couching their refusal in a demand that St. Clair should provide proof of his ownership of the table, which was of course impossible. The empty room was therefore very little used, but at the moment when Alamein threw herself into Rollo's arms, Winston unexpectedly walked in.

He gazed at his friend and his sister with a blank face and was about to beat a retreat when Alamein cried out:

"Rollo has asked me to marry him."

"Oh! That's the most marvelous news I ever heard in my life. You darling creatures. You are the two people I love best in the world. You angels. Do you know, I ought to confess that I have hoped for something like this ever since I invited Rollo to come and stay. I suppose you think I'm like a matchmaking mamma. And I've been so afraid, Rollo, that you were being held back by an idiotic materialistic feeling about money and responsibility and all that rot. It's glorious. And you've shown your sense of what really matters, Rollo, and your contempt for money in arranging to get married when you haven't a bean in the world. And you've chosen the right woman too, because Alamein doesn't care a hoot about money either."

Up till then Rollo had said nothing, but he felt it was time for him to assert himself.

"My dear chap. I'm awfully glad you're pleased. But you ought to be in the loony bin. Alamein will tell you that I am chairman and managing director of a company with prospects which extend beyond imagination, drawing a salary of three thousand a year and expenses."

"What on earth is this?" and Winston turned to gape at his sister.

"Well it's in prospect," said Alamein.

She would have liked to have asked Rollo whether he were really short of money, because, if so, she could offer him a loan, though there must be no more expensive jaunts to Paris. But she thought Rollo would prefer not to be asked in front of Winston, who was still baying with enthusiasm and showed no inclination to go away.

"Since the great secret is out, perhaps we had better go and ask your father's blessing," said Rollo, goggling at her. "We'll have to face the music some time, my pet." Having got so far he would have found any delay in clinching matters intolerable.

Alamein had been irritated by her brother, and it was to him that she addressed her first words.

"It isn't anybody else's business but ours. It's an entirely private matter, and I ought not to have blurted it out and wouldn't have done if you hadn't come in at the very moment when Rollo was proposing. All the same, since people are so infernally nosy, I'll come with you, Rollo, and tell St. Clair."

Winston was stung and startled by her words and turned scarlet. His sister's unprovoked attack was followed by her growling at him, as she went out of the room:

"And perhaps people will have the decency to let us alone after this."

"Oh Rollo!" exclaimed the unhappy Winston as the door closed behind his friend, "oh Rollo, Rollo, I've lost you, and Alamein is beastly and I was genuinely happy and not being selfish about it and now everything's made hateful. It's hateful and I want to die." Winston's eyes were filled with tears, and everything wavered as he looked round for a bed or a sofa or any damned piece of furniture on which he could throw himself and bury his face and sob. But the billiard room was bare. There was not a stick in it, and he found it a miserable, impossible business trying to weep while standing up.

It would not have consoled him to know that, only a minute before, Alamein had also looked about vainly for bed or sofa. The empty billiard room, with nothing but

69

a hard and dirty floor, was unsuitable for the extremes of joy and misery which require a recumbent posture. Winston rubbed the tears out of his eyes, blew his nose, and went off to tell Pash and Leela the good news if he could find them.

Meanwhile Rollo had told Alamein firmly that he would rather see her father alone, "as man to man."

St. Clair was busy correcting the proofs of his latest novel, the first that he had written in French, when Rollo knocked at the door and went in with rather a fatuous smile on his big face.

"May I speak to you, sir?" he asked.

St. Clair held up his hand—an impressive piece of flesh holding a gold-capped fountain pen and decorated with two gold rings. "Wait," he said.

Rollo sat down and waited, and St. Clair continued to read his own work smoothly and unhurriedly. Rollo had waited so long that it came as a shock when St. Clair turned to him and said:

"That word 'wait' reminds one of one of the greatest first chapters of any novel." Then, as Rollo's face registered blank incomprehension, St. Clair continued: "Mr. Baker, the first mate, is going through the roll call by the light of a lantern and comes to a pause—he can't read what is written. And a magnificent voice booms out: 'Wait.' Mr. Baker resents being told to wait, but he realizes it is the name he was trying to read: the name of the Nigger of the *Narcissus*—James Wait. That *malentendu* sets the key for all that follows during the voyage."

"I want to marry your daughter Alamein," said Rollo as St. Clair paused.

"So I was told. I am glad to hear it. So many young people dispense with marriage without reflecting that they are destroying the science of genealogy, or putting obstacles in its path. If you must have a lot of wives, follow the example of bluff King Hal. He, thank God, insisted on divorces. Otherwise we should all be Roman Catholics. If only Charles the Second, whose personal character I greatly prefer, had followed his example, we might have had a dynasty descended from Nell Gwynne, instead of those undistinguished Hanoverians—not that George the Third was altogether a bad man."

"I wanted to ask about settlements," said Rollo desperately.

"Well, that question is easily dealt with. There won't be any. You see, Alamein has about 800,000 from a trust set up by her mother."

"What was that, sir?" asked Rollo faintly.

"I said that Alamein has 800,000 a year. But what are your prospects, Mr. Kitson, since you introduced the subject and we are talking about money?"

Rollo didn't for a moment believe what St. Clair had said. It obviously could not be true. Even as a capital sum it would bring in an impossibly large amount. But she must have something. Making an effort, he turned to answer St. Clair's question.

"I hope to set up a company with your nephew, Signor Severin, to exploit his inventions."

"Splendid. That is admirable. It might take you a very long way." St. Clair opened his mouth wide and continued: "About fifty million miles. To think that my grandchildren may be moon maidens. Well, you won't be starting yet awhile."

"The first thing is to collect some capital. I was wondering if you would take up some shares. It is a chance to get in on the ground floor."

"Well in my experience other people always come along

71

and build on top of those who go in on the ground floor," said St. Clair, showing unexpected financial knowledge. "However, put me down for whatever you like, my dear boy. You understand these things."

Rollo had gone into St. Clair's study determined to get £10,000. These words tempted him, but prudence prevailed. "I thought you might take up 10,000 one-pound shares," he said.

"By all means," said St. Clair. "Ten thousand is a nice round sum. It will look very well in your prospectus."

Rollo got up to leave, but St. Clair called him back.

"You are a crossword wizard as well as a financial genius. Can you help me with this one: 'broad church navigator.' Fourteen letters."

Rollo bent over *The Times* and looked. "Starts with L. I should think 'latitudinarian' would fit," he said after a little reflection.

"Marvelous. I have faith in you, my boy . . ." said St. Clair. He would have said more, but Rollo had stepped into the passage and sought out Alamein.

"You have been a long time."

"Your father is delighted with the marriage. All went off very well. He tells me I am marrying an heiress. Is that true?"

"I hope you didn't believe him. What did he tell you?"

"He said you had 800,000 a year."

"Oh, that. Yes, Mother left each of us some money. I suppose it may work out about that."

"But that's an immense fortune," said Rollo.

"Old francs, you goose. Father always talks in old francs. About £500 a year after tax is deducted."

Rollo gulped. Still, £500 a year represented a capital of about £10,000. And if the old Jew coughed up another £10,000 it would be something to start on.

4

The day after Rollo had proposed to Alamein and been accepted by her and her family, he set off to visit Mrs. Standish Lorriner. The excuse for his abrupt departure might have been that the visit had been planned before his stay at the Château de Berri, that he had been invited for a particular day and that he did not wish to offend his hostess, a very rich woman to whom he was lucky to have been of use when she visited Cyprus in her yacht.

But in fact it never for a moment occurred to him that he might wish to stay with his bride-to-be, or that she might be disappointed by his leaving her within a few hours of her agreeing to marry him. He had carried out his program with the De Beaumonts with complete success and he would have found it tiresome to have to postpone the next part of his plan. For it cannot be imagined that Rollo would have gone to such pains to secure an invitation unless he had an object in view. It is true that this object had been altered by his agreement with Amadeo Severin; or, rather, it had not changed, but become more precise and indeed more important.

So directly he had had his English breakfast, he carried his bag down from his bedroom, put it in his car, kissed Alamein, waved a fond good-by to the assembled group of his future relatives, and drove south, taking the best Routes Nationales in order to reach his destination with the least trouble or distraction.

Les Oursins, on the tip of the peninsula of Juan-les-Pins, presented the formidable front to the outside world of a ten-foot wall covered with broken bottles which had been further reinforced by two meters of barbed wire. The gate was locked and barred, but an armed janitor appeared when Rollo rang the bell, and after he had given his name and it was found to be on the list of expected guests, the gate was opened and he was allowed to drive in.

The reason for these precautions was at once apparent: the villa was occupied by the very rich. Rollo was shown to his room; he had a bath, changed his clothes to a pair of canvas trousers, sandals, and an open-necked shirt, and went down to look for his hostess. She was not, however, visible, because it was only four o'clock in the afternoon and she always took a long siesta after lunch. Not finding her, he went into the garden, where a group of her other guests was sitting in the shade of a marble pergola looking over the sea.

A tall golden woman, with very blue eyes, dressed in dungarees, got up and greeted him.

"I'm Billy Tonson. I am only here while *Connie* is having her bottom seen to. Myrna asked me to look after you."

The meaning of her words eluded Rollo, and he could hardly attend while she introduced him to an older woman, Roma Palgrave, to Gundred, a sulky girl whose face was peeling, to Irma, a very beautiful one whose face wasn't, and to a fat man called Felix Hotchkiss.

Rollo realized that the woman was the wife of Sir Sam, but since she was perhaps a Sapphist and Connie her partner in perversion, he thought it might be better not to mention him. This was a piece of overtactfulness and turned out to be a mistake. Billy was in the habit of ringing up Sam whenever she was not at sea in the *Connie* and of having long talks with him. She had had such a talk that morning, at the end of which he happened to say: "I met one of your fellow guests here. He had persuaded Amadeo Severin, that extraordinary Italian boy I told you about, to start a company to exploit his inventions. I expect he'll try and sell you shares in it. Don't buy any. He's a big charming fellow, but a smoothie."

Thus forewarned, Billy said: "I think you met my husband at the Château de Berri." "Yes," said Rollo, uncertainly.

"What did you think of him?" This was awkward. Rollo thought that she was not living with Sir Sam, or that there was trouble between them, so after a pause he replied: "I thought he would be a hard man to please." That remark might result in confidences.

But Billy was annoyed. "Good God," she said, and turned away. But at that moment there was a scream like a peacock's and Mrs. Lorriner joined the party.

"Captain Kitson. I've forgotten your name! Oh yes, Rollo." Then screaming louder she addressed her guests: "This is my young friend—from Cyprus—wasn't it? He has left the army, he tells me, and is thinking of building a city on the moon. I can see you are all surprised. He isn't either Russian or American—but a very modest Englishman. When are you hoping to set off . . . Rollo?"

Myrna Lorriner was a woman who looked almost like a living skeleton. There was no flesh on her body, and a pair of glittering green eyes seemed to announce that she was a drug addict. Actually, she would have been a perfectly normal woman, but she was starved. She never ate anything and was in consequence so weak that she only spent six hours in the twenty-four out of her bed, or her chaise longue.

Thanks to her introduction, Rollo's reputation was soon

established and presented a good subject for conversation among his fellow guests.

"I'm certainly going! You'll put me on your first passenger list, won't you?" exclaimed the prettier of the two girls.

"You'll be sent there," said the fat man, Felix Hotchkiss, who was an expert on food and had promised to help Mrs. Lorriner's chef cook dinner the next day. He rolled his eyes dramatically. "Because I happen to know that there is a plan being worked out to get rid of our delinquents by firing them off in rockets to the moon. It is a revival of the system of transportation in use a hundred and fifty years ago. Undesirables were shipped to Botany Bay. That turned out badly, because their descendants, the Australians, come back. But you aren't likely to leave any descendants to populate Mr. Kitson's lunar city."

"Am I an undesirable, Felix?" asked the girl, standing up, holding out her arms and rotating slowly on the tips of her toes.

"Only morally," replied Felix.

"I think that it is a mistake to let our unwanted population come into existence. For that reason the pill is a much more satisfactory method than colonizing the moon or the planets," said Billy.

"It doesn't solve the question of what to do with Irma," said Felix.

"I would suppress you before birth," said Billy to the unfortunate girl, whose face puckered at this sustained attack.

"I think you are all awfully unkind," she said, almost in tears.

"So do I," said Rollo. "I have been thinking of going to the moon as a reward to offer."

"A reward for what?" asked Roma Palgrave, who had not spoken up till then.

"A reward to the people who have had sufficient faith in us to help us to build our city. A reward for the founders," answered Rollo.

"The reward might be not to go ourselves but to allow us the option of nominating someone—some unwanted member of the family—like my aunt Mabel," said Felix.

"You will have to build two cities. One for me and my friends and one for Felix's aunts," said Irma.

"I shall be most happy to oblige you if you will put up the money," said Rollo.

"You are actually share-pushing lunar stock within a couple of hours of your arrival—well, I'm damned," said Billy. She had decided to make Rollo's job harder.

"I can see he's a fast worker, and probably not only in business matters. So look out, Irma, you have been warned," she continued.

"Mr. Kitson and I are friends. We are going off to the moon together, aren't we?" said Irma.

"To the moon, honey?" asked Gundred, the girl whose nose was peeling.

"To the moon on a honeymoon," said Felix. "That will be the travel agents' slogan, and it will help to keep down the population explosion that is worrying Billy."

"Like Caesar, that captain of an earlier age, Rollo Kitson can engrave upon his waxen tablets 'weeny, weedy, weeky.' He has come to Gaul; he has seen what it contains, and he has conquered. Rollo Kitson, who bears one of the most noble names of Normandy, has borne arms in Cyprus and the Near East like the Crusaders before him. But it was not until he came to *La Belle France* that the Cyprian Goddess rewarded him with a bride of her own choosing and made in her own likeness, and he leaves tomorrow, taking with him not only our hearts but an investment of 10,000 with which to launch a project which we hope will bring fame and fortune to us all—and reward the moon goddess with a city of her own."

St. Clair de Beaumont paused, apparently expecting applause, but since none was forthcoming, he looked round his seated family and murmured rather huffily: "Well, if my feeble tribute is deemed sufficient, I shall say no more." Then, raising his glass of champagne, he cried in a loud voice: "I drink to the long life and prosperity of the happy pair; to my darling daughter Alamein and my son-in-law Captain Rollo Kitson."

"I rather advise you not to stay at the Regence if you go to Geneva," said *l'oncle* Mathieu, addressing Rollo across the table while the health was still being drunk. "It's a long way out of town, and you want to be in the center of things. I advise the Lion d'Or, which is only a stone's throw from the end of the lake."

Everything had gone as planned—indeed better than planned. Not only had Dr. Robert put up 260, which he said was all he could afford, but he had persuaded Sir Sam Tonson to put up a thousand. The only snag Rollo had encountered was that it looked as though it would be impossible to break the trust settlement and make use of any of Alamein's capital. But while he was paying his long-delayed visit to Mrs. Lorriner, he had succeeded in selling another 25,000 shares in Telefactors, divided between his hostess and his fellow guests. As a result he was in funds. But he kept his head in this unusual situation and began entering all his expenses in a small book.

And then came the marriage—and here they were with a couple of shoes clattering behind the MG, top raised now, and Alamein beside him in a quite wonderful Otterburn Tweed coat and skirt which would set all the chambermaids they encountered in Burgundy and the Jura mad with excitement.

Everything had gone as planned; everything had gone right—but there was one last thing that had still to come off. The first night with Alamein. For, owing to the speed with which all the other plans had been carried out, there had been no opportunity for the customary rehearsals of the wedding night. No matter. Rollo had thought about it. He had planned it thoroughly and well—not suspecting that nothing which has to do with love or love-making can be foreseen; that every gesture of love is in its nature impromptu and unarranged.

They had found a little hotel overlooking the higher reaches of the Seine, they had sat opposite each other, drinking an exquisite Montrachet and eating a couple of the most delicious fat trout plainly fried in fresh butter, and then, after a few crystallized white currants and a tiny cup of coffee and nip of Marc de Bourgogne, they had gone to bed. Rollo had refrained from lighting his pipe. Everything had gone as planned. Rollo had been tender, considerate, eager, ecstatic—and was asleep. But Alamein lay awake breathing deeply. She knew that in anything so intimate as what had just taken place there was likely to be a tinge of unpleasantness. Yet she realized that she had hardly been aware of it. She had been so occupied in being ready to respond. And then just as she was about to respond, it had all become strange and labored, and Rollo's great heavy panting body had lain inert while, still thrilled half through, she was waiting and watching not knowing for what—what angel should have come to the open door with a beating of myriad iridescent feathered wings.

And when it was no longer reasonable to wait and

79

watch, she realized that her limbs were stiff and that she was suffering a dull pain.

Quite early in her honeymoon Alamein learned that an essential part of physical love is the loneliness which follows immediately upon it. The act itself was pleasurable, even when, as sometimes happened, there was something vaguely unpleasant about it. But though she proved able occasionally completely to respond, her response was always short-lived, and loneliness followed. For Rollo, the life-giving act was always "rounded with a little sleep"; for Alamein, with a period of wakefulness, and it was in that hour, usually the hour before and after midnight, that she became aware of being completely alone in life. Lying awake in the darkness might have been more tolerable had Rollo's body been beside her, but he always clambered back to his own bed and became instantly unconscious. To overcome the irritation of her body, she got into the bad habit of thinking. Thus at the time when she should most of all have been nothing but a warm and drowsy animal, glowing with satisfied desire, she became entirely cerebral.

That lonely hour given over to analysis and speculation was, she believed, inevitable—not, of course, for all women —but certainly for her.

But what she found most difficult to accept about the act of married love was its complete separation from every other activity of marriage. Sandwiched between visits to the bathroom, those twenty minutes out of the twenty-four hours were spiritually water-jacketed and lagged with insulating material. Before marriage she had expected that they would have given color to every moment and that the act of love itself would be free to invade any hour of the day or night and not have been made to keep to a timetable.

But Rollo was, of course, a man who enjoyed organizing his life, and she supposed that his timetable was well planned. Thus Alamein's bed—always the right-hand one of the pair—was free from invasion except during the half hour after Rollo had finished brushing his teeth, and there was no unscheduled love-making before or after breakfast, or after lunch. In one of her wakeful periods Alamein came to the conclusion that if physical love were not what permeated and gave the flavor to marriage, money certainly was. For while sexual desire was not allowed to intrude, there was never a moment when financial questions—usually concerned with the strategy and tactics of launching Telefactors Ltd.—were ruled out as inappropriate.

Rollo was never happy unless he had planned everything in detail, and one of the delights of marriage for him was that he was now able to rehearse and discuss with his young wife all the steps he would take, all the letters and interviews he would write or seek in order to get the better of potential customers or backers. She on her part was naturally eager for the success of all such enterprises. On them depended not only Rollo's way of life and her own, but what was infinitely more important —whether Amadeo's visions and inventions could come true. Thus for the most part she got into the habit of being an eager and uncritical listener.

The choice of Switzerland for the honeymoon had been dictated by Rollo's decision to register the parent company in that country and to have subsidiaries in Britain and America. In that way Telefactors would enjoy low taxation and would be truly international and to some extent uncommitted. Rollo planned to make Geneva his permanent headquarters. He himself would have to spend a great part of his time traveling, flying from London to

New York and back to Geneva. Time would soon show whether this was a practical idea, but for the present he intended to take a flat or live in a hotel in Geneva, at all events until the parent company was established, with an office and a secretary. So they drove down from the Château de Berri through France, stopped for the first night at Aisey-sur-Seine, then went on by Dijon to the Jura.

They had lingered and loitered on the second day, spending a night at Verdun-sur-le-Doubs, enjoying the busy bustling atmosphere and the rich abundant food of the inn, which contrasted with the almost spartan perfection of the *haute cuisine* of the night before, where each morsel was cooked by the proprietor himself.

Then they had driven from the flat vineyard country to the Jura, which was Alamein's first sight of high mountains. That night they were to spend in Geneva. It was a brilliantly clear day when they reached the edge of the mountain country overlooking the Lake of Geneva and the valley of the infant Rhône. Rollo stopped the car; they got out, stretched their legs and stared. They were still in France but there at their feet was Switzerland, the lake, the city vaguely visible, and beyond innumerable mountains, Mont Blanc dominating everything to the south.

At the sight Alamein was seized by excitement: suddenly she knew that all would be well; that her marriage to Rollo, which had left her lying awake asking herself questions for the first two nights—that her marriage to Rollo was a miracle. She knew that all the plans, hopes, and dreams of her girlhood were piffle before the wind compared with the reality awaiting her, awaiting them both.

The sun was hot, but a faint breath of the distant glaciers and snow fields came, making her cheeks tingle.

82

With her eyes full of the scene she turned to look at Rollo. He was standing, a smiling, kind, serene colossus holding his pipe in his hands. She thought that she had never seen him so attractive. The mountain setting of mossy boulders and scattered pinewoods suited him, bringing out an unsuspected something that was heroic and Wagnerian. He was absent-mindedly scraping out the bowl of his pipe with a penknife, but he was contemplating the scene, not transported with enthusiasm, but silently drinking it in like stout Cortez. She was convinced that they had spontaneously felt the same emotion and were sharing it. As she leaned toward him he smiled, nodded his head, and tapped her on the shoulder.

"Damned fine. I call it bloody marvelous country, don't you, my pet? But we must be pushing along."

So much happiness, so much anticipation, so much relief overflowed that Alamein could not speak, but feeling sick and slightly dizzy got back into the car. Rollo had gone behind a tree but returned fastening fly buttons, then got in, slammed the door, and they began the long descent to the frontier.

Living close to another person makes it difficult to see him. Thus, just because they were so close, Alamein could not see Rollo, or Rollo Alamein. There was, however, this difference between them: she was trying to see him, while to discover her had not occurred to him.

For a week after they arrived in Geneva they lived in the hotel which l'oncle Mathieu had advised them to avoid. It was too large, too expensive, and too far away from the old town. By the evening Alamein was always tired from walking back to it twice during the day. The lake drew her with its great phallic plume of spray, and the market below the bridge excited her cupidity. She longed to have her own kitchen and to cook their meals.

83

Rollo spent his day in conferences with lawyers, with meeting bankers and inspecting empty offices.

One evening he took Alamein to a dinner party given by his lawyer, at which almost all the other guests were bankers or prominent industrialists and their wives. Rather surprisingly Alamein found herself far more at home in this company than Rollo. Conversation was in French and the subjects discussed were French books, French plays, French painting. Geneva is a curious island of French culture in which the inhabitants speak and think in French, hating the German Swiss of Bâle and Zurich, but are very definitely Swiss. Thus while Rollo was a stiff and awkward foreigner, Alamein was in a familiar atmosphere. Then, when she chanced to speak of her mother's frequent visits to Geneva in the days of the League of Nations, and was asked her maiden name, there was an immediate cry of recognition. One of the ladies, Madame de Windt, a Frenchwoman by birth, had been her close friend. Alamein had supposed that a honeymoon is no time for other people. But suddenly meeting Madame de Windt and hearing her speak with affection of her mother was like a spar for the shipwrecked sailor who has been washed overboard.

The spar to which she might cling was a tall woman between fifty and sixty with an amber skin and honey-colored eyes, gray hair which had once been honey-colored, a cool voice and disinterested manner, as though many years ago Madame de Windt had decided that her own life was a matter of secondary interest and had relegated it to the cupboard where she kept clothes of the outmoded fashions of her youth—objects of sentimental but no practical value, which perhaps ought to have been thrown away.

"I don't think it's possible to be happy in a hotel, do

you?" was one of the first things Alamein said to the lady. This sentiment expressed so strongly by a bride who was spending her honeymoon in one seemed to her gray-gold hostess to indicate that the marriage had not so far gone altogether well. Madame de Windt was too sensible a woman to be surprised. After all, it's only the first week of her honeymoon, she reflected.

"You don't like the Regence, then?" she asked.

"I don't think I can endure it another week. If only I could find a furnished flat. All I ask is that it should be old and that I should have a kitchen where I can cook. I can't get used to living in public."

Alamein left with an invitation to visit Madame de Windt whenever she was feeling lonely and with Madame's address and telephone number.

As they went back to their hotel after the dinner party Alamein discovered that Rollo was astonished at the accident of Madame de Windt's having been a friend of Marie-Thérèse du Bartas and of her remembering her so warmly after so many years. Perhaps it was because he was always planning to bring things about that he found it difficult to believe that they happened without contrivance. And meeting and making a friend of Madame de Windt was a very lucky accident, which went to show that Alamein could be very useful to him in ways which he didn't expect. For Madame de Windt was closely connected with important financial circles in Geneva—with just the businessmen whom he wanted to impress, but who had clearly not been very favorably impressed by the sound of First City in the Moon. He had spoken of it that morning to Roger Lampion, one of the youngest of them, and he had become terribly *terre à terre*. Roger Lampion had been at the party and was Madame de Windt's son-in-law. Yes, thought Rollo, it was certainly

85

one up to Alamein and to the De Beaumonts. Of course it was in a way one up to him too for having married her.

"Madame de Windt may be very useful to us," he said.

"Yes, indeed she will. She said that she would try and find us a flat," replied Alamein.

"I don't know why you can't be happy in a hotel where everything is done for you. But I meant she may be very useful to us in business and socially."

And then at a meeting with two Swiss bankers at the bar of the Regence, Alamein suddenly changed the whole tone of the conversation, which had been one of scarcely veiled suspicion. M. Duplessis, the younger of the two Swiss, had said: "It is at this stage really a question of automation rather than finance." Rollo tugged at his mustache, but Alamein broke in.

"That is exactly why my cousin, the inventor, and Sir Samuel Tonson are so keen on working together—'a job of programing my computers' is what Sam called it."

"Your cousin is a friend of Sir Samuel's, then?"

"Yes. My uncle—Amadeo's uncle—has known him for twenty years."

"It would make things easier if we could take up Sir Samuel as a reference," said M. Duplessis.

"Undoubtedly," said his older companion.

"Of course, old man, stupid of me not to suggest it," said Rollo.

A week after their arrival everything had been set in motion for the establishment of Telefactors as a Swiss company, but a delay was inevitable. Stock had to be sold, references checked. Rollo came back to the hotel in a jovial mood.

"Let's go off and explore the mountains."

An hour later they were in the MG making their way toward the St. Bernard. For a week Rollo proved to be a delightful companion, and Alamein felt happy with him. They drove slowly into the mountains, staying in little inns and spending one day climbing high above the road where they had left their car and the next scrambling down below it into a ravine where the glaucous glacier water boiled over the tumbled boulders and fallen pine trees blocked their way.

Alamein would wander away and pick a hatful of alpine strawberries while Rollo sat on a rock contentedly smoking his pipe. At night they would find lodging in a *Wirtschaft* and share a room in which all the plain deal furniture had been scrubbed and scrubbed again until the wood was white as bone and not a speck of dust was visible. In the morning, while the whole upland valley was still in shadow, there was the clanking of many cowbells as the herd was driven out to pasture. It was nearly autumn; soon the animals would be stabled in the byres for the winter and the snow would isolate the mountain village. Often their excursions took them up to the snow line, which came lower every few days.

For just over a week they lived happily together; the cool mountains making them feel that they were living faster and more vitally. The mountains, streams, rocks, cataracts, and alps stimulating them to physical exertion during the day and leaving them tired out and sleepily content by the time they came indoors for shelter and their evening meal. Bed usually followed at once—though on one occasion there had been a village dance in which they joined. Scrambling over rocks was less aphrodisiac in its effects than a day in the office, with cocktails before dinner and brandy afterward, and there were nights without love-making.

"What does the physical side of love matter?" Alamein asked herself. "One can be perfectly happy with it, or without it. *Je m'en fous de l'amour.*" There had been no difficulties or embarrassments between her and Rollo. They were sorry when the day came to go back to the city.

The day after their return, Rollo came back from consultation with the lawyer with a long face.

"He wants to put off the formation of the company until the bankers are definitely certain that American or British subsidiaries are actually being formed. This means that I have got to fly at once to New York. I hope not to be away for more than a fortnight or three weeks. Of course you will come with me." Rollo sounded uncertain.

"It would double the expense of the trip, and we certainly can't afford it," said Alamein.

"It would go on the expense account."

"It's not a justifiable expense. There's none too much capital, and it will be years and years before Telefactors starts to bring in a penny," replied Alamein.

"I can't bear to think of your having to go home so soon after leaving it," said Rollo.

"I shan't go home. I'll stay in Geneva. If I feel lonely I'll invite Pash to come and pay me a visit. And I'll find a flat."

"Brave girl!" Rollo had allowed himself to be persuaded and was rather relieved. He would enjoy more freedom if he were alone in New York than with a young wife to look after and introduce everywhere.

The following night he was gone, and when she got back from the airport, Madame de Windt called her up.

"Come round to supper. I've something to tell you."

Madame de Windt lived in a flat on the shores of the lake, overlooking, it is true, but little of the lake itself, though at least getting a glimpse of it through the trees bordering the lakeside drive. The curtains had not been drawn when Alamein arrived, and the thousand lights and their reflections visible through the branches marked out the opposite shore. The rooms themselves were rather overfull of heavy mahogany furniture, which while not at all smart was still comfortably opulent. To Alamein it was like home, for much of the furniture at the Château de Berri was also mid-nineteenth century.

"How lovely to be in a room like this," she said.

"Well I do hope you will think the flat I have found you will do. I feel sure you will like it—but I'm not so sure about your husband. Will you both come to look over it with me tomorrow?"

"I will, but Rollo can't. It will be a wonderful surprise for him when he gets back."

"Why where is he, then?"

"He's in New York."

Madame de Windt was certainly surprised, but all she said was: "Oh, my poor darling, how hateful for you."

"It's business, and very often that has to come first. It is a splendid thing, because now I may be able to take a flat and get it all ready while he's away."

Her hostess smiled at her and nodded her head.

"Well that's fine. Why don't you stay here tonight, in the spare room, instead of going back to the Regence, which you don't like? Then we'll go and look at the flat first thing tomorrow."

La Rue de l'Université starts with a flight of steps. Then a steep and narrow lane goes straight up the side of the hill between tall old houses. On the ground floors are shops—selling books, antiques, wine, embroidery.

Through a narrow arched doorway was a stone-flagged passage leading to a narrow turning stone stair on which it was scarcely possible for two people to pass each other. The houses and stairs were seventeenth century, but they might equally well have been, from their appearance, as early as the thirteenth.

Round and round they climbed, all the way up to the fourth floor, and there Madame de Windt unlocked the heavy oak door and led the way into a flat with one large living room, from the windows of which one could see the Vosges Mountains, their tops sprinkled with the first fall of snow. Besides this room there was a small bedroom, a kitchen, and a bathroom. Everything was perfectly fitted up, with a constant supply of hot water, a gas cooker, and electric fires.

Alamein had felt happy and confident from the magic moment when they had begun climbing the narrow medieval staircase and she immediately said she would take the flat. She stayed that night with Madame de Windt, but announced she would move to the Rue de l'Université next day.

"Hadn't you better stay with me until your husband comes back? You'll be awfully lonely there," said Madame.

"I am asking my sister, Pash, to come and keep me company." So no further objection could be made. It was curious, Alamein reflected, how even the nicest people always liked making objections to one's doing the obvious.

This generalization proved to be more true of Pasionaria than of Madame de Windt. From the moment that Alamein met her at the Cornavin station it was clear that Pash was in a state of ill-concealed emotion which was waiting for the first suitable moment to vent itself. They had scarcely got into the flat when she revealed that it was indignation.

"You must explain how this dreadful thing has happened," she declared.

Alamein was breathless. She had carried a very heavy suitcase up the four flights of stair and besides being breathless she was flushed with exertion. The tone in which Pasionaria had spoken would have annoyed Alamein at any time, but having to reply while she was out of breath and had a high color exasperated her. For her manner and appearance might have been taken for signs of embarrassment. And there was no reason for her to feel in the least embarrassed.

"What dreadful thing?" she gasped.

"Why Rollo's leaving you in the middle of your honeymoon."

"Don't be silly. Rollo hasn't left me. He had to go to New York on desperately urgent business."

Her sister looked at her with her keen black eyes and for a moment seemed to hesitate.

"Forgive me, darling. But are you sure that's the truth?" Then, as Alamein stared at her, she went on: "I can't believe that anything should interrupt a honeymoon. If everything is really well, you should have insisted on his taking you with him."

"He wanted to take me, but I persuaded him that it was far better that I should not go."

"That sounds crazy, darling."

"We couldn't afford it. Rollo's going was an inevitable necessary expense. My going too would have been a wild extravagance."

"Surely it's for Rollo to decide that, and not you. It's your duty to be with your husband."

"Why do you make such a fuss about a purely practical arrangement?"

"You are such a child. You don't seem to realize what you have done. You have broken up your marriage during the first three weeks. You are staying alone in a town where you know no one. You don't even know when your husband will come back."

If Alamein had got a touch of color in her cheeks climbing the stairs, her cheeks were now scarlet with anger. But as had so often happened in the past, her resentment led her to be silent, and she allowed her sister to point out that her behavior had been rash, unworthy of a young married woman, that it had betrayed a complete ignorance of male psychology and of what everybody would think, and that there was no guarantee that Rollo would ever come back from America.

At last, when Pasionaria paused in her admonitions, Alamein saw her opportunity. Looking her sister up and down and smiling, she remarked: "One would think that you were Aunt Fidèle," and she walked out into the kitchen to get tea ready.

Pasionaria did not allude to the subject again, for Alamein's words had struck home. She *was* being like Aunt Fidèle, and it was a grisly thought. She must find some way of disproving the accusation.

Nevertheless, though Pasionaria did not again raise the subject of Rollo's absence, she brooded over it in secret, asking herself: "Suppose he does not come back? Suppose he were *never* to come back? He has all that money that was given him to invest in Amadeo's lunatic invention. What is to stop him putting it in his pocket, changing his name, and disappearing? We could do nothing. We should never find him. If I were in his shoes, married to Alamein and with money in my pocket, I should be tempted, I must say. But if he were to disappear, how ghastly it would be for Alamein!"

The idea of Rollo's disappearance and the consequent wreck of Alamein's marriage, indeed of her whole life, had an irresistible fascination for Pasionaria.

So much so that, though it was quite obviously the wrong thing to say, she could not keep herself from hinting at the possibility of such a disaster when she met Madame de Windt the next day for lunch and they were alone together for a few minutes.

"You know, Rollo's going off in the middle of his honeymoon keeps reminding me of the stories of eighteenth-century fortune hunters who desert their brides after the first week; I suppose it is very naughty of me to think of my respectable brother-in-law in such a way."

"Very Freudian," said Madame de Windt in a colorless tone of voice.

"Oh, I do hope it's nothing like that," said Pasionaria.

Shortly afterward Alamein came back into the room and the subject was changed.

Rollo's first postcard had been lying at the Regence Hotel for two days before it suddenly occurred to Alamein to collect it. It was a colored postcard of the New York sky line, and it provided no food for Pasionaria's forebodings.

"My Darling Pet. Just arrived after long head-wind flight. Landed at Gander. New York quite wonderful and more than fulfilling my expectations. My address is Beekman Tower Hotel, East 49 and 1st. Love from Rollo."

After that, letters and postcards arrived almost daily and were invariably affectionate, cheerful, and optimistic.

Alamein showed them to Pasionaria and to Madame de Windt, and answered them with letters describing the flat, the staircase, shopping in the vegetable market, and the meals she cooked. Every morning, after a breakfast of rolls and coffee, the two sisters went down the precipitous little street with their baskets on their arms, crossed over the roads blocked with traffic, and walked beside the rushing water of the infant Rhône, which pours turbulently out of the Lake of Geneva, and then, descending some steps, found themselves in the market. All round them the vegetable stalls were heaped with immense roots of celeriac, blanched celery, ivory shafts of Swiss chard, purple kohlrabis, white tusks of chicory and curly heads of endive, bundles of black scorzonera roots tied up with wisps of osier. Then came stalls of fruit: apples, pears, quinces, medlars, and all the foreign fruits from Italy, and then stalls of plants and flowers. Inside the covered market were the butchers, displaying lovely thick roundels of steak trimmed for tournedos, poulterers, fishmongers, and dairymen, with their mounds of butter, pyramids of eggs, and all the cheeses.

Before setting out it was as well to have all the meals mapped out in detail and then to adhere rigidly to the plan. Both the sisters knew that—and yet how easy it was for the best of plans to be abandoned just because of a lovely little partridge, or a guinea fowl, or some particularly fat and gloriously spotted trout with powdered gold edging the silver of their bellies, there to lead the housewife astray.

In the flat the sisters talked English as they discussed Rollo and Amadeo, and Winston's aimless existence, and the comic aspect of Leela's relationship with their father. But directly they went down into the street with their shopping baskets they were Frenchwomen who spoke and thought only in the French language. But they were two Frenchwomen who never exchanged an abstract idea, who never so much as mentioned a book, or discussed a play, or planned to see an exhibition of pictures. They were only concerned with the dullest details of practical life, which, however, they seemed to find interesting.

Alamein's chief interest and excitement was in marketing and in cooking—but it was frustrated by there being nobody to cook for. It wasn't worth while to take trouble just for Pash. They did have a great occasion when

94

Madame de Windt came and brought an Englishman from the United Nations organization for refugees. Alamein served up a dinner which consisted of fresh trout fried in butter, steak *aux amandes* with braised celery, fresh green figs, peeled, in white wine with whipped cream. The figs were the second crop, from Sicily. Unfortunately Madame de Windt could not come every night, though after that meal she would have liked to.

One morning, as Alamein was contemplating a frustrating day, there was a loud knock at the door, and there was Amadeo, breathlessly apologizing for having arrived unexpectedly. He had not known the address of her flat, but had learned it from the Swiss lawyer whom he had just visited.

"Hurrah!" cried Alamein, kissing him on the cheek. "Now I have someone to cook for. Would you like a guinea fowl stuffed with green olives and chanterelles for dinner tonight?"

Amadeo always understood everything without asking for explanations. So he instantly understood Alamein's new passion for cooking, and after saying, "It's just what I was hoping for," he sat down in a deep chair to listen while Pash and Alamein poured out all the details of their lives during the last few days, constantly interrupting each other to deny, correct, or confirm what her sister had said. Actually the two girls had been on rather bad terms. For the longer Alamein thought about Pash's suggestion that Rollo might never return from America, the more meanly malicious it appeared. No doubt it had been said as a joke, but it seemed to her that it was a malicious, evilly disposed joke that never should have been made.

So Alamein had become remote and chilly, and Pasionaria, who was never chilly, had been resentful and bored and had begun to wonder why she was staying on in Geneva.

But the moment that Amadeo appeared, his eyes twinkling with complete understanding, everything was different. Even the past was changed and became interesting and amusing, and the two sisters, who had been too bored to speak to each other all the previous afternoon, vied in describing how fascinating life was in Geneva.

Later on, when that subject was exhausted, Amadeo told them about all the changes which had taken place at the Château de Berri in the week since Pash had left it. And then after a lunch of *pâté de foie gras,* hot toast, and endive salad, when they were drinking coffee, he let out that he would be staying at a hotel and not at the flat.

"But it's monstrous of you. We can easily find room," the sisters protested in unison. But Amadeo was adamant.

"Later on I shall try and find myself a room not too far away from this street—for Geneva will probably be my headquarters for the next few months."

Alamein went off to plan her cooking, and Amadeo took Pash with him when he went to find himself a room and drop his bag at a hotel. As she stoned the olives and cleaned the orange wood mushrooms, for the first time since her marriage, Alamein was in a state of wild joy. The whole prospect of life had changed. Amadeo was going to be living close to them in Geneva. He would be able to explain everything to Rollo and see that he didn't make a mess of things. And almost every day she would see him; he would drop in, his eyes blinking and twinkling, rubbing the tip of his nose with the palm of his hand in that extraordinary way, understanding everything and wanting no explanations.

Pasionaria returned fairly early in the afternoon alone.

Amadeo had a business appointment and would come back in good time for a drink before dinner.

"It is hopeless trying to get onto human relations with any of one's relatives," said Pasionaria. Alamein was busily rubbing butter into pastry and folding and rolling, folding and rolling again. She was going to provide homemade *croissants* for Amadeo's breakfast the following morning. He would have to come round first thing from his hotel.

"It's a waste of time," said Pasionaria. "This thing about incest has gone so deep that even a boy like Amadeo, who is no blood relation whatever, is terrified of having any intellectual intimacy with us."

"I should say that is just what I have with Amadeo," said Alamein languidly. She was listening to Pash now and observing her.

"Well, you may, since you've become a married woman and are no danger. But Amadeo's scared stiff of me. I suppose it's not only because of the connection by marriage, but because he's really a 'queer.' "

Alamein was holding herself tightly. "You had better explain about that," she said in a faint voice.

"Surely you must have noticed that Amadeo is homosexual? I think I've always known it. It is certainly obvious enough when we go bathing in the river. And lately he and Winston . . ."

"I must get back to the kitchen," said Alamein. But in the kitchen she sat twisting her apron in her hands. Could what Pash had said be true? No, of course it wasn't. If she had "always known it," if it had been "obvious enough when we go bathing in the river" she would have talked about it years ago—*ad nauseam*. No, it was clear that she had invented all that. Nevertheless, *it might be true*. Even though Pash was lying, *it might be true*.

And of course Winston . . . God damn that foul sister of hers.

Amadeo came back in plenty of time, and they had an *apéritif* before dinner. But everything had gone wrong. The guinea fowl was falling off its bones and the braised celery was stringy and everything was disastrous, and Alamein saw clearly that Pash was just a witch.

Nothing could have spoiled the cheese. It was perfect, and so was the coffee and brandy that came after. But it was not until then that Amadeo said:

"Aren't you excited that Rollo will be back the day after tomorrow?"

Alamein and Pasionaria cried out together.

"I telephoned him, this afternoon when I felt sure I should catch him. He sounds madly pleased with himself, but God only knows what he has let me in for."

"And he told you he was coming back tomorrow?" asked Alamein.

"Not tomorrow. The day after. As a matter of fact, I told him that he must come back at once."

"And did he agree?" asked Pash.

"Oh yes, he agreed."

Pasionaria rather regretfully said that since Rollo was returning she supposed that Alamein would not want her to stay. It was the kind of remark that is not easy to answer, and Amadeo was filled with admiration for the skill with which Alamein treated it.

"Darling Pash, I can never thank you enough for coming to keep me company, and may I call on you again whenever Rollo dashes off somewhere and leaves me a grass widow? But you see you were wrong. He has resisted the temptation to abandon me. Why don't you fly? The plane leaves for Paris at four o'clock in the afternoon."

5

The four of them sat round a solid mahogany table in a room at the lawyer's. Rollo, Amadeo, Alamein, and Monsieur Plotz. The latter gentleman had never met any of them before that morning, when he had been nominated by La Banque Universelle et Helvétique as their representative and had been enthusiastically proposed as a director by Rollo and elected unopposed because it seemed to Amadeo and Alamein to be too rude to inquire into his qualifications. But at all events Monsieur Plotz, being a total stranger, did impart a touch of formality into what might otherwise have been a family party. To add to the importance of the scene there was an English-speaking stenographer sitting at a side table, ready to take notes. The proceedings were carried on in English because Rollo was not at all fluent in French.

Alamein, who had been summoned to attend the board meeting while washing her hair and had not got it dry, was on her best behavior. It was her first experience of business. Amadeo kept striking thin Italian wax matches on his thumbnail to light a cigarette which he immediately let go out.

"I shall make my account of my trip purely factual. I shall avoid the personal except insofar as my personal life is also my business life," said Rollo, leaning back in his chair at the head of the table.

"I went to New York, to Detroit, and I had invitations

to visit Cape Kennedy, but I rather reluctantly canceled them in order to report the position before making large commitments, which would have been difficult to avoid. Well the position is this: First City in the Moon is regarded as a very long-term proposition, and the U.S. Treasury is the real obstacle. In fact, one very important rocketman, a general in the U.S. Air Force, told me that we could have done damned well with it during the early part of the Eisenhower administration. If we had put up the project immediately after the first sputnik, the President and the American people would have jumped at it. But space is no longer in the forefront. The emphasis is on space for defense rather than on space at large, for its own sake. No doubt enthusiasm for space will come back, but for the present First City in the Moon is out.

"On the other hand, I have two eager buyers for Automatic Armies—one an African republic and the other the representative of Generalissimo Chiang Kai-shek."

"I haven't yet made a telefactor tank," said Amadeo. Rollo held up his hand.

"If I may, I'll finish the report of my trip first and then we can have a discussion, and you can say what you like. O.K.?" And he looked with benign superiority at his fellow directors.

"I am quite ready to admit that selling an automatic army to the African republic may be a trifle tricky. It would be all right as to price and as to payment: they are exporters of diamonds and gold. The snag is that I had a tip that they would use an automatic army to wipe out all the white people in Rhodesia and the Union of South Africa."

Amadeo opened his mouth but was at once overwhelmed. "Later, if you don't mind. Well I did nothing to discourage the African. Indeed, I think that I promised him priority. However, I think that it's most unlikely that we should be allowed to deliver the goods. But, you see, it doesn't matter—because the Formosan government is, if anything, more eager. And it is always useful to have two eager buyers bidding each other up. If at the last moment the U.N. forbids delivery to Africa, we can always ship it to Chiang—at the price the African would have paid."

"Have you discussed price, then?" asked Monsieur Plotz.

"Yes. I suggested fifteen per cent over the subcontractor's price, plus management charges and bank charges on capital employed, plus a fee for training experts to direct the army, which would not be less than three million dollars. That is for a fully automatic tank brigade. I said that while we were certain to have teething troubles, we were sufficiently advanced to sign a contract with the subcontractors within six months."

Amadeo laughed, but Rollo ignored it and went on. "Turning from Africa to Asia. As I said, the Formosan government is even keener than the African. In fact, we provide the only possible solution to Chiang Kai-shek's dilemma, which is that his army is becoming senescent: the average age of his troops being fifty-four. Moreover, the Chinese Communists have shown themselves adept at brainwashing their prisoners. I believe eighty per cent of the American prisoners captured in Korea co-operated to some extent with the Communists, and no doubt the proportion in Chiang's army would be almost one hundred per cent. But, as I pointed out, you cannot brainwash a tank. Machines are immune at present from ideology.

101

Nor can our kind of tank be captured and used against us. It will only obey its master's voice. Therefore it can only be smashed, or put out of action.

"Well all this appeals enormously to the Formosans, and they are so keen that they instructed their representative in Geneva to get in touch with me immediately. He did so this morning, and I have invited him to meet me informally at dinner for a discussion tonight."

Rollo looked at his wrist watch and added: "Any comments?"

"On behalf of La Banque Universelle et Helvétique I would like to emphasize the security aspect of our discussions. Though we are a strictly commercial undertaking, engaging in perfectly legal activities, it might, from a security angle, be wiser to go under a camouflaged name—both in our interests and, still more, in those of our customers. I suggest that we drop the title of Automatic Armies and call our subsidiary company something like Terrestrial Telefaction."

"That seems common sense," said Alamein, to the surprise of the other members of the board.

Monsieur Plotz proposed and Alamein seconded the change of title, which was carried.

Amadeo suddenly looked at each of the others in turn and said: "On behalf of the inventor of telefaction, who will have to attempt to implement your promises to the bloodthirsty, I should like to remind you that although I can guarantee to adapt one tank to be operated by telefaction in about three weeks after I am given it, the problems involved increase enormously when we come to deal with the deployment and operation of a large number in the field. It is quite impossible to work out the details necessary without the use of the very latest type of electronic brain, which does not exist in Europe.

To do the job at all will involve a first cost of about two million pounds for equipment and, even so, it may be ten years before it is possible to translate theory into the actual operation of a whole army corps from staff head-quarters many hundreds of miles away. By that time the average age of Chiang Kai-shek's troops will have put most of them into their eternal dugouts. Moreover, what you seem to have concealed from Chiang and African alike is that automatic armies are completely out of date. They can't stand up to a nuclear bomb, even though they are immune to the effects of fall-out."

"That's why Chiang is so anxious to get an automatic army to reconquer China before the Chinese Communists have stocked up with the bomb."

Amadeo laughed a little scornfully.

"You realize I can do nothing, except produce a sample tank or car, until I have a laboratory costing about six million dollars?"

"Your equipment is a stile we shall have to get over when we come to it," said Rollo. "It's bound up with making a big sale. I shall give Professor Wu a sketch of what telefaction can do at dinner tonight. Then we shall arrange a demonstration at a time convenient to him and to Signor Severin."

The dinner was held in Rollo's flat, and the dinner itself was cooked by Alamein. The choice of the flat was for the sake of security: there was, as Rollo explained to his guest as he drove him from the office to the center of Geneva, no possibility of the rooms being bugged and the conversation being recorded by the agents of an enemy power.

Professor Wu, who was a nervous man, thanked him profusely for the precautions.

He was a tall, thin, pale man, with white hair cut

en brosse and a feeble little white mustache, who wore dark glasses and a white waistcoat with glass buttons. Rollo introduced him to Amadeo, and he made polite noises and accepted a dry Martini. He then took a seat, and Rollo said: "Signor Severin will now tell you something about his revolutionary invention."

Professor Wu nodded politely, and Amadeo began: "Telefaction is the discovery of how to transmit power through space. It is not the transmission of signals through waves, like wireless; it is the transmission of power—power measured in thousands of kilowatts—from any point where it is available to any spot where it is to be used, with far less wastage than occurs in the transmission of power from a generating station by cable. The uses of my discovery are prodigious. It will revolutionize industry in peace. It may possibly enable mankind to explore the planetary system. I wish to continue to control the early stages of the exploitation of my discovery, and that is why this small company has been formed.

"You, however, are only interested in its military application. So I will say that by combining my invention with up-to-date methods of remote control, I can operate a tank—lacking fuel or a crew, and therefore able to carry more armaments. If such a tank is captured, it will be entirely useless to the enemy, since it can only be operated by means of power transmitted to its electric motor by telefaction. In a couple of years' time, if my researches are adequately financed, I could put several thousand such tanks into the field and equip them to be operated entirely automatically. I can give you a demonstration of the principle tomorrow morning. If you can give me an order, I will go ahead with it. If you do not, I may abandon the military application and explore the civilian uses of my invention."

104

The professor nodded his head and said rather shyly:

"Your invention has reminded me of a sport we used to indulge in in China—the flying dragon kites which fight one another while their friendly owners are holding the strings safely on the ground in a garden below."

Amadeo leaned forward and said: "That is the kindest and best thing that anyone has said to me about my invention. It has often occurred to me that if there were two automatic armies, the generals could get a lot of fun out of them, and do less mischief than they have always done in the past."

"I think you and I look at things in rather the same way," said Professor Wu. "It seems that some men always want war. Thanks to your invention they can fight a war by proxy—and let peaceable men like us get on with the work that interests us. In my case it is that I am engaged in translating the great American poet Whitman into Chinese."

Alamein came in, was introduced, and led the way to the little dining table. When they were seated, she looked round the table. Amadeo and the professor were entirely taken up with each other and with their thoughts. Monsieur Plotz was astonished and slightly shocked and quite out of his depth. Rollo was genially tolerant, even approving.

"Tell me about Whitman. I've never read a line of him," he said.

"Whitman is the soul of America. He is the American man, the expression of the spiritual effect of the empty fertile prairies and forests of the New World on the English and Dutch pioneers. Whitman is spiritual and anti-intellectual. He expresses the spirit of masculine America. Whitman's life spans the nineteenth century and hinges round the Civil War in 1862, when he was a man of forty-three. He spent the war working among the wounded in hospitals. He idolized Lincoln. His poetry shows his passionate love for freedom, space, democracy. His voice recurs in American literature. There is a touch of Whitman in most great American writers, thinkers, and politicians. In all the writers who have remained American: in Mark Twain, for example. It was from the spirit of Whitman that Henry James and T. S. Eliot fled to England in order to receive the O.M. and devote themselves to the perfection that appeals so much too much to a Chinese. All our art has been of that kind—carved on jade."

The professor's soup was cold. Rollo recalled him to realities. He swallowed it down, asked for more, and swallowed that. But while Alamein was bringing in the roast guinea fowl he began again.

"Whitman appeals to the masses. It is for that reason that I believe he will be acceptable in China today. I do not speak only of those of us who because we were born too early are refugees in Formosa today, but of the masses in Red China.

"Yet there is a strange paradox: in many of his poems Whitman is curiously Chinese in spirit. Here is a poem of his which I have translated, and some of my Chinese friends tell me I must have found it in Po Chü-i I," and he recited:

Cavalry Crossing a Ford

A line in long array where they wind between islands
They take a serpentine course, their arms flash in the sun
Hark to the musical clank.
Behold the silvery river, in it the splashing horses loitering
*   stop to drink.*

Behold the brown faced men, each group each person a
picture, the negligent rest on the saddles
Some emerge on the opposite bank, others are just enter-
ing the ford—while
Scarlet and blue and snowy white,
The Guidon flags flutter gaily in the wind.

Monsieur Plotz looked at his empty plate, but Professor Wu continued, unaware that they were waiting:

"There is thus the happy paradox that while Whitman often speaks in language and form acceptable to Chinese people, he also appeals to the new spirit and to the Chinese mind, and will show America is spiritually a democracy and not a plutocracy. For my work in translating Whitman I have here a Guggenheim fellowship."

Professor Wu was still talking about Walt Whitman when they had drunk their after-dinner coffee. But at last Monsieur Plotz shook his cuffs and half rose.

"I must apologize . . ."

"Not at all," said Rollo, waving at him to be seated.

"I was about to suggest to Professor Wu that you are a very busy man of business and that he should return to the subject of an order for Terrestrial Telefaction vehicles."

"Certainly," replied the professor. "I was instructed to ask for a demonstration of the telefactor tank before passing you our order."

"That would involve a considerable delay, wouldn't it, Amadeo?"

"Not in principle. I haven't got a tank, and doubt if I can borrow one, but I can demonstrate telefaction with my own car tomorrow. In a day or two I could demonstrate it with a motorboat on the lake. The principle is exactly the same as with a tank. But I cannot get a license to drive a tank through the streets of Geneva, and if I did so it would cause embarrassing publicity, which I feel sure the Formosan government would wish to avoid."

"I understand perfectly," said Professor Wu.

"Well come along and get into the driving seat tomorrow morning, Professor," said Amadeo.

A Citroën two-seater is very unlike a tank, but is, however, capable of driving over rough ground. Professor Wu hung back.

"The lady will take the driving seat. I have no license to drive."

Alamein slipped in behind the wheel, and Professor Wu took the seat beside her, but before they set off, Amadeo explained that in case of difficulty they would be able to telephone to him direct. The little car was fitted with a short-wave set.

They waited while Amadeo went back to his control room, and Professor Wu had begun to ask Alamein about her tastes in world literature; then suddenly they were off.

The sensation of sitting in a car driven by remote control is peculiar: rather like the difference between traveling in a trolley car and in a bus. Alamein had experienced it before and felt no fear. Soon the baby Citroën was bowling along the double road which leads to the European headquarters of the United Nations. It kept well in to the curb and traveled at about thirty kilometers an hour. Alamein sat with her hands folded so that Professor Wu could see that there was no deception. Suddenly he seized her by the wrist, and she realized instantly that he was in the grip of fear and not of lust. He wasn't making a pass at her. And then a huge American car with a

Negro driver swirled past, cut in as close as possible, and jammed on its brakes.

For a tenth of a second Alamein sat in frozen horror, feeling the crash coming. Then the brakes of the Citroën came full on. Her head and Professor Wu's head bumped the windshield, but without breaking either the skin or the glass, and as they recovered themselves, they realized that the little car had not crashed but was executing a right-angle turn, climbing over the concrete, shrub-planted division between the two roadways, and was on its way back toward the center of Geneva.

"They tried to make us crash: they want a police inquiry," said Professor Wu.

Alamein looked back. The big saloon car had gone on. Then she saw it far behind, waiting to turn after them at a road intersection.

"Who are they?" asked Alamein.

"I don't know. I have not seen them before," replied the Professor. The telephone rang, and Alamein heard Amadeo saying: "There is a large American car with a Negro driver about three hundred yards behind you and rapidly overtaking which will try to provoke a minor collision. I want you to hold tight to your seats."

A moment later his voice came again to say: "Put your arm out, Alamein." The little car started to swerve into the middle of the road, in front of their pursuer, then cut back in to the curb and stopped suddenly. The big American car had brushed past them and gone ahead. Then it also pulled in and stopped. A Negro got out and began walking back toward them.

"If you are satisfied with the demonstration, Professor Wu, will you get out and take a taxi?" said Amadeo over the wireless telephone.

The Chinese professor did not need to be told twice;

109

he jumped out, ran across the lane of traffic, stopped a taxi going in the opposite direction, and disappeared.

"You can take over driving, Alamein. I don't think there will be any more trouble," said Amadeo over the telephone. "I suppose it was Professor Wu they were interested in." He was right; Alamein drove the car back to the Rue de la Cité and was not followed.

A few days later the Formosan government agreed to buy a specimen automatic tank and, if it passed their tests, within six months to buy four hundred others. Professor Wu went back to translating Whitman.

The Formosan government's option put Rollo in great spirits. But Amadeo at first was horror-struck. "Of course I can produce one tank in six months, but I can't possibly produce four hundred in under ten years, even if I have a ten-million-dollar laboratory," he said.

Rollo grinned. "My dear chap, they'll never take the option up. Long before we are due to deliver all of the four hundred, something new will have wiped out all thought of automatic tanks."

"That's true," said Amadeo.

"Meanwhile, let's go ahead in getting the sample one ready. I bet Monsieur Plotz is astonished. I think my contribution helped Professor Wu to make up his mind, don't you?"

"What was your contribution?" asked Alamein.

"The big car trying to crash you," said Rollo, laughing.

"By golly, Rollo, your chaps damned nearly did crash my little Citroën," said Amadeo.

"You mean to say that you arranged for the other car? But that wasn't honest, Rollo," said Alamein.

"Don't be such a silly kid. If you ask me, it was pretty obvious salesmanship. But since we were lucky enough to draw a professor, it worked. He didn't want any nearer

110

acquaintance with his black brothers from the Congo, and must have sent in a marvelous report."

"I think it was because he and Amadeo liked each other," said Alamein.

"May well be," said Rollo generously. "But we've booked our first order. So far so good."

A fortnight later, when Alamein had taken her basket and gone down to the market by the river, Rollo called Amadeo.

"I would like a word with you about streamlining our organization. Come along to the office in half an hour." For some reason, the words "streamlining our organization" annoyed Amadeo. There was, he reflected, no organization at present. There were the three of them and a representative of the Swiss bank. He kept the appointment feeling irritated and rather bored.

"Look here, Amadeo," said Rollo, scraping out his pipe and proceeding to fill it slowly, and speaking solemnly: "I've been wondering whether it's worth your while being a director. You see, you are really the brains of the whole concern—that is, the technical adviser. But it's wasting your time, and actually it's inaccurate, to describe you as a director. You don't want to waste your time at board meetings dealing with day-to-day details."

"What is your idea exactly?" asked Amadeo, beginning to feel rather angry.

"Well, I suggest you give all your time to research and to the technical problems facing us—and to do that I suggest that you resign from the board."

Amadeo agreed in his heart that the board meetings were a waste of time. But the assumption that he could give his time to research when he needed a ten-million-dollar computer before he could really do anything exasperated him.

"I won't agree to that," he said firmly. "We started this thing together as partners only a few weeks ago, and I shall certainly not agree to change our relationship. I insist on remaining a director." There was a pause, and then he asked: "What does Alamein say about this?"

Rollo had not consulted her, but he had no intention of saying so if he could help it. He slowly lit his pipe and decided to give up the attempt to oust Amadeo for the moment.

"Well, if you insist, and if you take that tone, I have no more to say," he said sulkily. "Only you are really the technical adviser and I wanted to free you from work that is a waste of your time."

"I appreciate your motives," said Amadeo with a smile. "Is that all you wanted to see me about?" Soon afterward he left the office and went down to the lake. He was planning to buy a boat and was in a happy frame of mind. But Rollo was feeling angry. He had realized that he would have to raise the question of directors' fees with Monsieur Plotz very soon. The bank had already intimated that it would keep the books of the company and look after the cash. It would be more likely to agree to reasonable fees if there were only three directors instead of four. It would save money; Alamein would not query his proposal, Amadeo might well do so. But the chief thing was that if he could get Amadeo off the board, he would avoid having trouble with him later. He would be under orders and would not be able to start interfering with policy.

The question what did Alamein think about it was typically maddening. He ought to have anticipated that. And he had better tell her something before Amadeo told her. Otherwise it might be a bit of a mess.

After dinner he beckoned to Alamein to come to him

112

on the sofa, put his arm round her, and nuzzled the lobe of her ear. A little later he said: "I have been worrying a bit about Amadeo wasting such a lot of his time here in Geneva when he ought to be doing research. And I rather put my foot in it. I saw him this morning and told him that because his research was the first priority, I felt we ought not to insist on his being a director and wasting his time attending meetings. Of course we could always call him in when something special arose. So I suggested that he resign from the board. But he absolutely refused to consider it. I don't know if you would like to put it to him."

"I think it was a completely crazy idea of yours," said Alamein. "First of all, he has told you a hundred times he can't do any more research without the equipment he needs. Then how could we make decisions without him? He knows so much more than either of us does. Besides, it would spoil everything if he weren't here. . . ."

Rollo pushed Alamein away and stood up.

"I just can't understand your attitude, Alamein. I am thinking about the good of the show. . . ."

"But surely you can see it would be monstrously unfair to have Amadeo slaving away to produce things without knowing what we were planning to do with them? The whole point is to help his genius to realize itself . . . not to take advantage of it."

Rollo went out of the room and slammed the door. The office which Rollo had chosen for Telefactors S.A. was situated in the least attractive part of Geneva—in a big block about halfway between the United Nations buildings and Cornavin station. Thus it was neither on the edge of the city, nor in the old part, nor near the lake. It was on the first floor, reached by an elevator, and consisted of a large impressive room, which was the board room and Rollo's office, and was equipped with a board table and six chairs, a large desk with a swivel chair, and a big low armchair for visitors. Besides this room, there was a toilet and a very small room fitted with a big steel cabinet and typist's table and chair.

The board room was for Rollo: the little room was for Amadeo. But a few days after his failure to get Amadeo to resign, Rollo decided to make it difficult for him to frequent the office. The obvious thing to do was to engage a secretary and to put her in Amadeo's cubbyhole. But he would have to justify the secretary, because for the time being he did not write more than three letters a day. Until the inquiries about Telefactors began to pour in, he had to occupy his time, and also to occupy the secretary. He decided, therefore, to write a book: a popular exposition of telefaction and of the changes it would bring into the world.

"You will have to give me some of the gen—though I shall avoid technicalities as far as possible," he said to Amadeo.

He did not seem to resent it when the inventor of telefaction treated his suggestion as a joke.

"We have got to open people's eyes and get them talking. It doesn't matter whether they understand what they are talking about. How many people really understand the principle of space travel, or even of a jet engine, or of television?"

"How are you going to explain my invention in popular language without going into technicalities, so that your reader is made to think he understands something?" asked Amadeo.

"By analogies, of course. I shall explain that, just as in the telephone, it all depends on the multiplier; that your

114

invention is in its essence the discovery of a new multiplier and transmission at very low temperatures."

Amadeo was impressed. He had forgotten that in one
of his first conversations with Rollo he had used exactly
the same phrase.

About a fortnight after the book had become one of
Rollo's accepted occupations, Amadeo went to the office
to fetch a notebook in which he put down ideas which
occurred to him. He was walking across to his cubbyhole
when Rollo stopped him.

"I'm awfully sorry, Amadeo old man, I think I have
made a bloomer. You and I will have to pig in together
for a bit until the book is done. You see, I was such an ass
as to engage a secretary without thinking where I was
going to put her. She's absolutely first class. She's just
what we shall need when things start humming: bilingual
and all that. It didn't dawn on me that she would need
a room. So I have bunged her into your room. I'm trying
to get a room upstairs for her if I can. But for the time
being she's installed in there. Of course this room is as
much yours as mine until we can make some other arrangement."

Amadeo nodded his head and walked in on her.

"I've left some of my possessions in here. Do you mind
going into the next room while I collect them?" He held
the door open and shut it after she had gone out. Then
he opened a book and read it for half an hour just to
make Rollo feel worried. After that he collected his possessions: some back numbers of *The Nation,* a few cata-
logues, some notebooks, and a box of letters.

Then he picked up an armful of his books, put his
head into Rollo's room, and said to the young woman:
"Will you carry this lot down to my car? Here is the
key."

115

The girl gave an appealing glance at Rollo, but he was looking for something under his desk, so she took what she was given and went out. Amadeo sat down in the big low armchair opposite Rollo's desk—a chair which had been arranged so as to make visitors feel psychologically helpless while talking to the chairman of Telefactors S.A. After a moment Rollo looked up, but Amadeo was leafing through his box of letters.

"Really I'm damned sorry it should have happened this way. It is one of those things . . ." said Rollo.

"I shall do my work on my boat. In some ways it will be much better. My correspondence will not be disarranged," said Amadeo. He looked up and met Rollo's eye.

But before anything further was said, Mrs. Zapatecas came back into the room.

"There is a gendarme who seems worried about your car. I did my best to pacify him, but perhaps you had better go down," she said to Amadeo. There was no gendarme, and as far as Amadeo could see no place along the straight road where one could have hidden himself. Amadeo reflected: She invented that gendarme. Rollo is right. That woman really is a good secretary.

Amadeo's boat played a continually greater part in Alamein's life. It was at hand on the lake, so that visiting it was not like trailing out to the office and arriving tired and footsore. For of course Rollo took the car to his office first thing every morning. And when she got to the office she was in the way and felt that the expensive secretary thought that she was spying on her.

"Why shouldn't I have been your secretary? I'm bilingual and I can type, after a fashion," she had protested when she first heard of the girl being engaged.

Rollo had been firm. "You don't understand, darling.

You are my wife and you are also a director. That's bad enough, but if you were my secretary too it would give us away as a one-horse show."

"Isn't it paying rather a lot for prestige?"

"I admit Dolores—you don't mind my calling Señora Zapatecas by her Christian name, do you?—I admit she is expensive and seems like an extravagance. But she is certainly worth it."

"Do you mean to keep her on after you have finished your book?"

"It all depends how things develop. I don't believe in crossing bridges before you get to them."

But on the boat it was bliss. It was a sailing cutter with a big open cockpit, a large cabin, and a tiny galley with a gas cooking stove. One of Alamein's pleasures was cooking—but her gift was wasted on Rollo, who was always miserable unless he ate in a restaurant. He had given up coming back to lunch and took Alamein out in the evening, unless they were giving a little dinner party, which was a rare event.

So Alamein provided lunch for Amadeo on the boat. It was one of those wonderful late autumns when the sun is as hot as summer. There was usually enough wind for them to sail without using the auxiliary motor, and Amadeo would anchor off a rocky lee shore, because he said it was there that you found fish. And surprisingly often he did catch a fish, and then Alamein would fry it in butter and squeeze lemon on it and, when it was cooked, split it down the backbone so that they could have equal shares.

Sometimes he ran the boat in to a jetty on the French shore and they landed just to feel they had been in France, or for Amadeo to buy a packet of Gauloises.

They both liked the French tricolor better than the Swiss cross and, though they quite liked Geneva, they were each in a rather childish way nostalgic for France.

Driven out of the office, Amadeo made the boat his home, and gave up his room and slept on it.

"You won't be able to go on all the winter," said Alamein.

"There may be no winter. Haven't you heard Rollo say that he didn't believe in crossing bridges before you got to them."

"But there must be a winter."

"I somehow don't believe we are going on here," replied Amadeo.

The three were on odd terms. None of them knew quite what they were. In the evening Rollo would ask Alamein what she had been doing all day, and she would say: "I went out in the boat." Then Rollo would say no more. It didn't occur to him to be physically jealous. But he did deeply resent the fact that Amadeo had never asked him to go out sailing with him. He had asked for an invitation.

"Nothing I like better than mucking about in a boat. We must go out together. I was a wet bob, you know."

"Oh were you? In that case you ought to buy yourself a boat. We could race each other," replied Amadeo. Rollo had installed a typist in his room without telling him and had looked through his letters, and he was not going to be unduly friendly.

The curious thing was that Rollo minded and Amadeo didn't care a straw. Rollo loved Alamein and he respected Amadeo. He was proud to be associated with a chap who might change the world just as Marconi had changed it, or that Scottish chap Baird, who invented television and had got nothing out of it. But he could only love the one and respect the other on his own terms—if they accepted his values, which were self-evident to him. He couldn't accept theirs. Yet all the time in a curious way he would have liked to accept them. And he and Alamein were on odd terms too.

They loved each other physically. They often looked at each other almost gloating over each other's good looks and splendid bodies. They enjoyed looking at each other like that in public, and Alamein felt the heat run over her body and her nipples growing hard. It was like undressing in public, and it excited her. So they looked at each other in the restaurants or the night club that Rollo sometimes took her to, and it was like daring each other to go further, and though they never spoke they knew each other's thoughts. Alamein became skilled at this game. She would visualize what she would do with Rollo's body, exactly how she would do it, exactly how it would be, and put it all into her look, so that often Rollo could not bear any more. He would sigh heavily, turn away, and call: *"Garsong, garsong."*

But when after silently baiting each other with lust in public they went home—then often enough it was not so good. When it actually came to making love, Rollo's splendid body wasn't so good. He was curiously clumsy and heavy; his love-making never lasted long enough. So Alamein was seldom able to do what she had visualized so vividly. When she was wanting more and more, Rollo would look at her with love in his eyes but a little shamefaced and exhausted, and on one occasion he said: "Enough is as good as a feast." And then he kissed her again and climbed out to his own little bed. Only as it wasn't enough, so it wasn't a feast or as good as one.

All the same, Alamein never completely admitted Rollo's faults as a lover to herself. She avoided thinking about

119

them as much as she could and she never looked at another man with the slightest interest, unless it were Amadeo. He was the only man who could ever possibly be her lover, or could have been, supposing she had never met Rollo.

Amadeo stayed on his boat as much as he could, and Alamein came every day. It had got too cold for swimming, so he did not see her naked, or nearly naked. And he loved her so much that everything was perfect when they were on the boat. He never touched her except to hold out his hand to help her as she climbed out of the dinghy. They talked quite naturally about Rollo: they did not avoid mentioning his name, but they never discussed him. Amadeo never told her that Rollo had read his letters.

And except once a week, at the board meeting, Amadeo seldom saw Rollo. "Come in tomorrow and give me some gen for my book," Rollo begged. "But of course, I should love to," Amadeo answered. But he forgot to go, or if he remembered, it was too late when he was the other side of the lake.

Alamein had remembered, but she did not remind Amadeo of his appointment. There was plenty of time for the wretched book. She never dreamed of feeling jealous of Mrs. Zapatecas, but she hated the book and didn't believe in it. It seemed to her that if anyone were to write one, it should be Amadeo. One day she told Rollo that. She was afraid that she would hurt his vanity—but not a bit. He explained to her that it was natural she should think so—it seemed obvious—but the obvious was usually wrong in advertising.

"If Amadeo tried to write the book, he would be trying to explain things which none of his readers would ever really understand. He would be too difficult and at the same time too condescending. But I don't completely

120

understand telefaction myself, so my reader will realize at once that I am not condescending. He and I are equals setting out on a difficult adventure together. Everyone will read my book, and the science critics will say it is a little masterpiece."

Alamein realized that Rollo was probably right—but all the same, the fact that he should be right annoyed her, and she was nettled. Why should everything have to be advertising? Why should the lowest standards always prevail? It was not what she had planned when she had brought Rollo and Amadeo together. And suddenly she found herself saying: "Of course that is true for the kind of people you want as readers. But there must be some serious worth-while people in the world who really want to understand what is happening in the world and have the intelligence to do so. They can't all be just phonies like you and me, pretending in order to get by."

"You need your eyes opened to realities, my pet," said Rollo in a strained voice. He felt insulted, not by being called a phony, but by her comparing her intelligence with his own. Her next remark did not help to smooth matters.

"No. It's your eyes that need opening. You don't realize that there is a residuum of educated people in the world. And that they are the ones that matter." It was a phrase of St. Clair's that she had appropriately remembered.

Rollo had no wish to start a quarrel on the eve of going out to an important dinner, but her words were too much, and he was just about to tell Alamein that she was a silly woman when there was a knock on the door.

Alamein opened it. Her brother, Winston, was standing on the threshold. She stared at him blankly for two or three seconds before stepping back and letting him enter the flat.

"Has something happened?" she asked. For only as the bearer of catastrophic news—as the messenger in a Greek play—could his presence be explained. Meanwhile Rollo surveyed him gloomily from over her shoulder. They had been on the brink of a quarrel, and the unfortunate Winston played the part of a lightning conductor between two clouds charged with electricity.

Faint gestures of welcome could not be avoided, but these were quickly overlaid with the questions:

"Why are you here?"

"What has happened to bring you here?"

"Is everything in a state of chassis, old boy?" So that almost at once poor Winston was having his story dragged out of him.

Pasionaria had been perfectly beastly to him. She had been making mischief with St. Clair.

"Really, that sister of ours is a dirty-minded swine."

And so he had jumped into the little secondhand car he had bought himself and, having nowhere else to go, had headed for Geneva.

Alamein agreed with her brother about Pasionaria. But there were practical details to be settled. Rollo and she were dining out with Madame de Windt and meeting the Swedish ambassador and the representative of an African republic at the United Nations—both of whom Rollo classed as useful contacts.

"We are just going out to a dinner. Have a drink." Rollo poured one out.

"Cheers. Come and have lunch with us tomorrow and tell us all the dirt. I'll make an effort to get back here at one o'clock," said Rollo.

Winston had been counting on spending the night—all the nights while he was in Geneva—with them. He was startled and almost on the point of tears. Alamein, suddenly angry, would not help.

"Why don't you look up Amadeo, old bean?" said Rollo. "He almost always comes ashore for his dinner, doesn't he, Alamein? What's the name of the dump where he eats?"

Alamein found herself forced to give directions.

"Come on, mustn't keep Madame de Windt waiting. See you at lunch, old bean," said Rollo, leading the way out.

A flash of decency led Alamein to stop and say: "Stay here as long as you like, and if you don't find Amadeo . . ."

"Hurry up, my pet," called Rollo from the winding stair.

Next morning Amadeo dropped in to say that Winston wasn't feeling well enough to have lunch. He had been sick in the night. Alamein looked hard at him and knew that he was lying, but he went away without replying to her question: "What's the matter really?"

There had been hours of tears and impassioned outbursts.

"I won't speak to either of them. Their food would choke me. They would never have met if I hadn't invited Rollo to come and stay when he hadn't a penny. I was genuinely overjoyed at their marriage. But they have never said one word. Never sent me a postcard."

Half an hour later it would start again.

"That foul beast Pash does at least care. Alamein and Rollo are like wooden dummies. And Rollo called me 'old bean'!"

"I suspect he always did call you 'old bean,' only you've forgotten," said Amadeo.

"I know you don't like him. But he was, or I thought he was, someone quite wonderful. And whatever you may feel about him, he's *brave*. And that means a lot to me," said Winston, snuffling loyally.

"I quite agree. He has buncombes, as I believe Leela once said. Buncombes in more senses than one," said Amadeo, laughing. Leela's remark had become a family joke.

"But you must pull yourself together, *old bean*," said Amadeo, and he ruffled Winston's hair as he uttered the painful words. "You see, even if you don't go to lunch with them, you have got to face meeting Alamein here on the boat this afternoon. She usually comes out to the boat in the afternoon, and you have got to be brave and have buncombes, even though she is your sister."

There was so much kindness in Amadeo's voice that Winston had to laugh.

He had indeed looked at Amadeo adoringly and said:

"But you are so kind. Nobody has been kind to me."

Tears had trickled down his healthy cheeks, but Amadeo had said with rather less kindness: "Now enough of all that."

Of course Amadeo was right. He would be brave. And by the time Alamein came aboard he had forgotten his self-pity and had almost forgotten that he had a grievance against her.

"I suppose you wouldn't come to lunch because Rollo and I were so beastly to you. But we were in a foul temper with each other when you turned up. And really you ought to have given us warning."

From anyone other than a member of his family Winston would have accepted this apology, but not from his sister. Alamein, he felt, had never been one to preserve

124

the decencies, and now she was dragging open his wounds and sprinkling salt on them.

So he didn't respond. Presently Alamein asked him how they all were at the Château de Berri.

"Just as hellish as usual—only a bit more so," he replied.

Alamein laughed, and Winston glowered at her and said:

"Nothing to laugh at in that. You've got away and forgotten what it's like."

"Oh no I haven't. But possibly distance lends enchantment to the view."

"It wouldn't seem enchanting to me even if I were up in your moon city. Anyway, I'm not going back there in a hurry."

It dawned on Alamein that Winston had installed himself on the boat. But for how long? She thought it wiser not to press him about his plans, and he did not vouchsafe any more information. It was a dull windless day, and after a much shorter stay on board than usual, Alamein asked Amadeo to put her ashore. Winston remained on board, and for the first time there was an opportunity to speak.

"Tell me what has happened," she said, and she had a feeling of dread while she waited for Amadeo to reply.

"Winston is going through an emotional crisis. I expect he'll pull round soon. But I am a bit worried. So for the time it's best for him to keep me company on the boat."

"What really is his trouble?"

"That is a very long story, and I don't think I really know. But what seems to have happened is that Pash went and told St. Clair that Winston was trying to seduce Leela."

"I daresay he was, you know," said Alamein.

125

"Quite possibly in a semiunconscious sort of way—or vice versa. Leela may have been trying to seduce him."

"Yes, I think you are right there. But what did St. Clair do?"

"He told Pash to mind her own business. Unfortunately he then told Winston what she had said and that he wasn't taking any notice of it. Winston dashed off and knocked Pash down, and they both did a lot of screaming. St. Clair then told Winston that he had better go away until he could control himself better."

"Did he hurt Pash?"

"I don't think so."

"What a pity."

Alamein walked around the streets for a time depressed by the shop windows all full of expensive things that she didn't want. There were thousands of watches, and surely one good watch, or two at most, would last a lifetime? She wore her mother's watch, a large gold one which had been converted to a wrist watch and which kept perfect time. Pash had refused it because it was not elegant enough. Of course the watches might be useful if there were enough rich people to wear them, but everything else was expensive and unnecessary. Really all she liked about Geneva was the lake, the old streets, and the market full of vegetables and fish and meat and everything one wanted to eat.

Now that Winston had come she would hardly ever be able to see Amadeo alone. She had lived for those hours she spent with him on the boat. Suddenly she remembered what Pasionaria had said. "Amadeo is homosexual. . . . And lately he and Winston . . ." It was almost certainly true. Pash had a fiendish power of discovering things. It had not mattered whether Amadeo were a homosexual or not as long as she could see him and

126

sail with him. But now *she would not be wanted on the boat*. She had been necessary when they were sailing —or at any rate a great help. Now Winston would loose the jib sheet when the boat went about. Somehow that was worse than his sleeping in the same cabin with Amadeo. Because the deck and the cockpit of the little boat were what she had been enjoying almost every day: they were hers. But she had never slept in one of the bunks. And if Pash were wrong—she had never believed she was right before—surely Amadeo would not put up with that wretched creature her brother? Yes, he was a wretched creature—but he was horribly good looking. That certainly was true. And she would have to wait, and it might be a little while before she could be sure. But of course it was true, and she was a fool who was trying to blind herself.

She decided that evening that she would not visit the boat the next day. She would wait for Amadeo to invite her.

Rollo asked about Winston, but some feeling of delicacy or family loyalty prevented her from giving him the whole story of Pasionaria telling her father of Winston's attempted seduction of Leela, or, what was more probable, Leela's seduction of Winston. Those two had always been inclined to hug each other and to exchange lover-like kisses.

"Oh, Pash and he had a frightful row over some nonsense and he hit her and then they screamed at each other and St. Clair told Winston to clear out if he could not control his temper."

Alamein kept her resolution not to visit the boat the next afternoon and then again the day following. That night she could not sleep, and in the early hours said to herself: "I am behaving like an utter ass. Amadeo's friendship is what matters to me more than anything in the world. I have wounded him by being unkind to Winston. So now I must set out to show that I love him. I will give a dinner party and invite Amadeo and Winston to meet Madame de Windt, and I will ask the Zapatecas woman, to make the numbers even."

"What's the idea?" Rollo asked suspiciously when she proposed her plan next morning.

"Well, I simply have got to do something about Winston. After all, he *is* my brother. I thought if we asked him to dinner we should have done what was required."

"O.K., my pet. I'll tell Dolores to keep an evening free."

Alamein sent out invitations, they were accepted, and the day of the party arrived. She had arranged it in order to be nice to Winston and to please Amadeo, but she realized that it was likely to be an awful occasion. Señora Zapatecas was an unknown quantity and might turn out to be socially embarrassing; Winston was emotionally unbalanced, unpredictable, and not averse to making scenes; the relations of Rollo and Amadeo were strained.

Fortunately Rollo had insisted that the dinner party should take place in the private room of a little restaurant almost opposite their flat, to which they would adjourn afterward for coffee and brandy. Alamein was therefore free from worries about cooking and serving the meal and could devote herself to her guests.

To her surprise the evening turned out to be a delightful family party. Señora Zapatecas was an amusing talker and made herself very agreeable to Amadeo. Winston was looking very handsome and was wearing a smartly cut dark-blue dinner jacket. Moreover, he was relaxed, unself-conscious, and friendly with everyone. Madame de Windt took an immediate liking to him and talked to him practically all the evening.

128

Rollo and Alamein, hostility suspended, were left to watch how much their guests were enjoying themselves. After returning to the flat they all settled down, and conversation went on until nearly midnight. Before the party broke up, Alamein heard Madame de Windt inviting Winston to lunch for the following week, and as Rollo helped her on with her mink coat, preparatory to driving her and Señora Zapatecas back to their homes, she said to Alamein in a voice loud enough to be overheard by Winston in the sitting room: "What an enchanting man your brother is, darling. Why have you kept him hidden away? I must make the most of him while he remains in Geneva."

It was not a passing fancy, and the attraction was mutual. Winston was very soon spending half his time in her house. Alamein never saw him except on two occasions when she went there. But Amadeo came to the flat—usually with a note for Rollo containing answers to questions which were needed for the book. Once he came with a present of fish which he had caught in the lake. Alamein began to cry after he had gone away, looking at them and thinking that she might have been there when they were caught. Then later on, while she was cooking them, she scalded herself with hot fat and was free to curse. She could not bear giving way to tears, but rather liked using filthy words. The fish were responsible for both.

When Amadeo had come in, Alamein had asked: "How's Winston? How does he spend his time?"

"He's looking for a job," was the reply. It was on the tip of her tongue to say: "Not very hard, if I know Winston," but she suppressed it because she did not wish to seem harsh or critical in front of Amadeo.

But a week later when she asked, "How's Winston getting along?" she received the answer: "He's got a job."

Madame de Windt had found it for him, and he liked it. He was salesman in a picture gallery, where his perfect French and English and fair German and his excellent appearance made him just the young man that the proprietor, whose French and English were execrable, wanted. And Winston had become enthusiastic about painting.

Amadeo did not add that Winston was no longer living on the boat because he thought that Alamein knew it. It was a fortnight before she found out—from Mrs. Zapatecas, during a visit to the office—and she felt bitterly wounded because the other woman knew it and she supposed that Amadeo must have concealed it from her deliberately.

In the meantime Rollo was stuck with his book. Question and answer would never solve his difficulties. He did not know the right questions to ask. The book required Amadeo's collaboration or supervision, and Amadeo was no more willing to collaborate or supervise than Rollo was prepared to have him back in the office.

Dolores had dug herself in, and Rollo was already dependent on her. He could not live without an objective, and it was clear that sitting talking to Dolores in Geneva and waiting for custom to come would never get them either to the moon or, what Rollo wanted much more, to their being offered an acceptable take-over bid, with a fat job for himself, on the payroll of the taker-over.

So it was clear to him that he must go to America again, and if the Americans wouldn't play, to Moscow or Peking. The notion of the Chinese Reds having telefaction ought to make the Pentagon cough up the dollars. And the wonderful thing was that what he was selling could be written on a sheet of paper—it was just the know-how. Amadeo kept on bellyaching about his ten-million-dollar computer.

He wanted it just to play about with it himself. Let the purchaser buy the computer and jigger around with the damned thing. Rollo had come into telefaction in order to sell it to the highest bidder and to get a big job for himself—preferably in public relations or market research, or labor psychology or one of the newer rackets. He must waste no more time, but get cracking. He would start with New York, but if there was no market there, he might end up in Indonesia, Malaysia, Rhodesia, or the Congo. The idea of selling it to the blacks and then seeing how well they could program Amadeo's ten-million-dollar computer made him laugh.

It would mean leaving Alamein—but he would find her waiting when he got back. He wondered if he could be as sure of Dolores? He could not possibly take her with him; Monsieur Plotz would throw a fit. He had already told Rollo that Genevan businessmen did not go to night clubs as much as the Americans or the Japanese, and, in any case, they never took their wives with them. No, taking Dolores wouldn't look well, though she was a charming companion. If he were bound for Cuba she could come along, and Castro would fall over himself to buy. Unfortunately he had nothing but a million tons of molasses to buy it with.

Possibly he could persuade Plotz that Dolores was the right person to stay and hold the fort—and with a rise in pay to suit the added responsibility, she would probably stay.

Rollo was a man whose weakness was in moments of sudden temper, and Alamein precipitated one after a dinner at which he had drunk more than usual.

"How long will it be before Amadeo can get the computer he needs? You talk about his giving his time up to research, but that shows you don't understand the position. Sir Sam offered to let him use any of his computers, but they are not good enough. He must have a ten-million-dollar one. That is the only thing that matters. How long will it be before he gets it?"

"You are crazy if you think he'll ever get one," said Rollo sulkily.

"What do you mean? What else are you working for?" asked Alamein.

"Well, if my plans work out, we shall scare the American government, or the Russians, and they will buy us up."

"What will happen then?"

"We shall be in the money. I mean millions."

"Well that would give Amadeo his opportunity to start a laboratory and buy any kind of computer he wants."

"Not bloody likely. Can't you see that what we have to sell is either Amadeo himself, in which case he works under their orders, at what they want, or else, if they don't want him in their team, we sell a restrictive covenant on his future activity."

"But you can't do that," said Alamein, staring at him as though she had never seen him before.

"And why can't I?"

"Because it's not fair. It's the meanest thing I ever heard of. You can't really want to do such a thing."

"You must try and grow up, my pet. It's what I'm going to do when I get to America."

"No you won't."

"Why not?"

"Because Amadeo and I have as much voice in what is done as you have, and we won't agree."

Rollo jumped up, knocking over the table with his glass on it, and rushed out of the room and out of the flat.

132

Next morning he came out of the bathroom newly shaved, scented with Old Spice, and greeted her at the breakfast table with:

"I talked a lot of crap last night, my pet. I get worried. You see, we must raise a lot of money in order to make a show. And we are in a strong enough position to make almost any terms we like, and of course Amadeo's work and equipment will be in the forefront of our terms. But it will take a lot of money, and it is no good nagging at me and making me mad."

Alamein accepted this apology rather stiffly. The memory of what Rollo had said the night before was not forgotten.

The beautiful warm days of an exceptional October were ending. Geneva shivered as the snow crept down her circle of mountains: in the morning fog covered the lake. In the market, where three weeks ago Alamein had hesitated between the little sweet green figs and the larger purple ones, which had more flavor, to go with the slices of smoked *prosciutto* with which she and Amadeo used to start their picnic lunches, the figs were gone. So were the *fraises des bois,* and the wood mushrooms. Her life, which had been as rich as the market stalls, was now as poor as they. So when Rollo announced that he was planning to leave for the United States in a few days' time, Alamein accepted it almost without asking why it should be necessary again so soon.

"I suppose you'll be able to get Pash to come and keep you company, my pet?" said Rollo.

"I don't think so. You know she has got herself a job. Besides, I think I would rather go back to the Château de Berri and see how Father's getting on."

"Well, that would be fine. Dolores is going to stay on

and hold the fort. She'll forward my letters. There's no reason why you should stay here while I'm away."

"All right then. I'll send a note to Leela tonight to tell her to expect me."

There was a formal board meeting to approve Rollo's departure. Alamein found herself sitting beside Amadeo, whom she had not seen for a week, a week which she had felt was like a month. She turned to him and said, before the meeting started:

"I'm going home when Rollo leaves."

"So am I, directly I've laid up the boat for the winter." The meeting started, but Alamein paid no attention to what was going forward. At the end, when it was breaking up, Amadeo asked:

"Why don't you let me drive you back?"

"Thank you very much. That would be wonderful."

Alamein went to the airport to see Rollo off and to drive his MG back to the garage where it would be stored while he was away.

And when the plane had taken off and had disappeared into the sky, what a relief! The last kiss and the last look of love as he called, "Good-by, my darling! Good-by, my pet!" had been squeezed out of her and there was nothing left but the relief of being alone.

Alone and not alone. For Amadeo was waiting for her to help him scrub out the boat, jettison perishable stores of food, stow away the sails, paint metalwork with grease so that it would not corrode. Winston was too busy in the gallery to help with the dirty work, she supposed. Women were needed for that, even by homosexuals.

All the same, she loved working with him and being allowed on the boat. They did not talk about anything except the immediate future, the job in hand, what they would find when they got home.

One would have thought that Amadeo would have been eagerly excited about the future of the company; would have been wondering what Rollo might succeed in accomplishing on the other side of the Atlantic. Not a bit. He seemed to have forgotten his inventions and to have put Rollo out of his mind as though he had never existed.

When the boat was laid up, Alamein had to tidy up her flat and lock it up. But before their departure they received a message from Monsieur Plotz: would they come to see him at the bank?

It was obvious from the first moment that he was worried, and he was the kind of man who is slightly unpleasant to other people when in that unfortunate state of mind.

"In the absence of Monsieur Kitson, I must ask you what you propose doing to rectify the balance of Telefactors S.A. at the bank."

"But surely, Monsieur, that is your province? I believe that you were appointed a director of the company with responsibility for its financial relationship with the bank," said Amadeo.

The long and short of it was that the account was overdrawn. Monsieur Plotz had agreed to Rollo's taking with him sufficient funds for a period of extensive travel. There were various sums to be paid out for the electronic equipment which Amadeo had ordered for the equipping of the prototype tank for the Formosans. And there were Mrs. Zapatecas' wages and the rent—though those items were, Monsieur Plotz conceded, a mere bagatelle. But money was wanted urgently. Rollo had said that Monsieur de Beaumont had not paid for all the shares allotted to him but would do so whenever required. Alamein said she was going home and would ask her father to send a check. This pacified Monsieur Plotz, and his manner was more civil at their parting than at their arrival, though it was still that of a man in distress.

Before she left Geneva, Alamein accepted an invitation to dine with Madame de Windt. The only other guest was Winston, who arrived shortly after her. But while the ladies were still in the hall, her hostess said: "Your brother has real genius: he works tremendously hard, and I feel very proud of being able to help him. What is so amusing is that Roger, my son-in-law, refuses to come to my flat or to meet him. The Genevans are so stuffy. What is so funny is that it is a liberation for me. And now you must see how Winston is redecorating my flat."

The effect in the drawing room which overlooked the lake was startling. Winston had stripped the walls of Lincrusta, had had them replastered and covered the wet plaster with reeds pressed flat with hot irons and afterward enameled or varnished until they shone like rods of brass. The ceiling was a very pale blue. Against the background of reed there was hung on one wall an abstract picture by Klee; in the other corner a mobile of metal shapes and wires vaguely reminiscent of the three crucifixions on Golgotha, executed a slow but imperfect pirouette.

Unfortunately Madame de Windt still retained most of her late nineteenth-century furniture: solid mahogany side tables, a sofa upholstered in rep, a massive piano, and heavy chairs.

The dining room was less discordant, for there Winston had contented himself with stripping the walls of their dun-colored paper and replacing it with pale-blue linen, while on the floor lay a magnificent Aubusson carpet patterned in blue, gray, and terra cotta. Winston arrived as Alamein was being shown it, and she was able to praise what he had done as genuinely and wholeheartedly as Madame de Windt could wish.

Directly Winston appeared, Alamein was able to see that that lady, while retaining her warm friendliness and common sense, was head over ears in love. More surprising, it seemed to Alamein that her brother was completely unembarrassed and appeared genuinely to like her. He was staying in Geneva until he had finished her flat: he had great plans for the chief bedroom—but they were a secret. "Something in the style of a modern Giulio Romano, inspired by the idea of space travel and the first city in the moon," he said confidently, and then laughed.

It was a new Winston, whose existence Alamein had never suspected until that evening: a handsome, confident young man who set out to amuse the ladies and did it very well. He told them anecdotes of his new job and of the visitors to the gallery who refused to admit being baffled by abstract paintings and of how after he had triumphantly sold one of them he was berated by his employer because he had held it upside down in ignorance.

"But upside down it will have to stay, because they would certainly not keep it if we confessed to my mistake. Not that I am certain that it was a mistake and that old Blumenfeld is right." And then, with a quizzical glance at Alamein, he added:

"My father, who has experience in such matters, says that truth is relative and that what is generally believed comes to be true after a time—anyhow as far as history is concerned—and I would add abstract art."

"Madame de Windt must have known our father when she was a friend of our mother's," said Alamein.

That lady spoke of him without enthusiasm and asked if he were still writing.

137

"Yes indeed," replied Winston. "His latest novel, written in French, was published last month, and St. Clair is confident that he would win the Nobel Prize with it except that he has enemies in Scandinavia."

Alamein burst out laughing, but Madame de Windt held up a reproving finger.

"You are forgiven this once—but you are not to curry favor by making fun of your father."

"I will try never to do so again," said Winston. "But why do you forbid it?"

"Because it is cheap—a cheap boomerang that may come back and knock you senseless when you least expect it," she replied.

It was not until the evening was over and Alamein was walking up the steps leading to the Rue de la Cité that she suddenly thought: Now I can begin to understand why Amadeo is in love with him. I always thought it was an aberration from which he must recover. Now I see that he is probably right.

She had laughed at Winston's jokes; she had been delighted that Madame de Windt was so much attracted by him—apparently even more than a little in love with him. She was overjoyed that his decorations should show originality and taste. But because of her sudden revulsion, she felt inferior to the brother whom she had thought of as an embarrassment and a problem for the last few years. He was a handsome, brilliant boy on the threshold of success. She herself was a wretched creature, scarcely even a woman yet—a useless girl. Amadeo was quite right to prefer her brother, and because she idolized him, she had involved him in an unfortunate business relationship by means of a silly marriage. What she had done might turn out to hamper his research. She had done it all for nothing. And her marriage was pointless.

138

That night Alamein lay awake feeling, not jealous of Winston, not resentful that Amadeo should love him, but deeply humble and ashamed of herself. She promised that for the future she would put all selfish thoughts aside and would try to undo any mischief that she might have caused by her marriage. All she could hope was that she could protect Amadeo's work from Rollo's commercial plans.

6

Next morning Amadeo set off with Alamein to drive to Château de Berri. She had looked forward to the physical pleasure of sitting beside him, of hearing him talk, and of watching the winter landscape unroll itself before them. But it was a bad day. They had climbed almost to the top of the hill above, and had come to the snow lying among the trees and in patches at the side of the road when Amadeo pulled up.

"I'm sorry, I shall have to go back. I forgot to leave money for Winston." He turned the car round, and they began driving back to Geneva. Alamein said nothing. It seemed to her that anything to do with her brother took precedence with Amadeo, and in her depressed and humble state of mind she was not prepared to resent it, or even to suspect that it might be otherwise. It was the way things had worked out.

Amadeo drove first to his hotel, then to his bank, and then to the gallery where Winston was at work. Afterward, as they headed back toward France, Amadeo said:

"Winston is finding it very hard to live in Switzerland. He is only earning a miserable pittance at the gallery, and although he was promised a commission on what he sells, Blumenfeld makes excuses and puts off paying him. So I am giving him something to go on with until he finds his feet."

"I am so glad. I mean I am glad you like him and are

taking an interest in him," said Alamein, who wanted to say something nice.

"He told me he had dinner with you at Madame de Windt's last night. Did you see the decorations he has designed for her flat?"

They discussed the decorations, and Alamein described how charming and amusing Winston had been during the evening. It seemed to Amadeo as though it were impossible for her to talk about anything except her brother: whatever he said she brought back to Winston. He did not suspect that she was hoping that he would make some confidence which would enable her to say that she was so glad that they loved each other and that she hoped that Winston made him happy—and all sorts of things like that which were not in the least true, but which perhaps would lead to an easier relationship.

They had been driving for some way in freshly fallen snow, and suddenly, on a hairpin bend going down a steep hill in the forest, the car went out of control, skidded, and then very slowly went into the rail which bordered the ravine below them. While this was happening they sat perfectly still. The wooden rail cracked, but held the little car, and Amadeo was able to open the door on his side and get out. Then Alamein shifted across to his seat and got out also. The right-hand side of the car and the right front wheel hung over an abyss.

Amadeo had caught hold of her hand as she was climbing out; directly she was on her feet he drew her to him and kissed her.

"That seemed to last a very long time," she said, referring to the skid.

The little car was balanced on the very edge of the mountain slope, held by the cracked wooden rail. Alamein leaned in while Amadeo held her and rescued a basket

141

in which she had put food for lunch. Then he locked up the car and they set off down the road to look for help.

The virgin snow crunched under their feet. They were the first to mark it, since cars were waiting for the snowplow and nothing had been along the road since the night before. The sun shone; the frosty air seemed to burn up their lungs with each breath. Between the bent snow-laden branches of pine they could see the white stretches of rolling land below. At a hairpin bend there was a drift, and before Alamein had realized it, she had gone in over her knees. Amadeo pulled her out, and soon afterward they stopped to eat their sandwiches and drink the Valais wine, sitting on a heap of gravel after they had brushed off the snow. Soon afterward the snowplow came grinding up the hill, and by the time they had finished their meal and left the forest a string of cars was passing them on the way to Switzerland. They were absolutely happy; immersed in the moment. But the moment passed. They reached a farm, where the farmer agreed to go back with Amadeo and haul the car onto the road with his tractor. Meanwhile Alamein went on down the road to the village, where there was an inn in which she waited.

It was very clean, the walls of polished and the floors of newly scrubbed pine boards. The place smelled good. There was a big heating stove glowing in the middle of the room.

By the time Amadeo arrived it was dark and it had already started to snow again.

"Better stay here. It is a lovely place," said Alamein. So they stayed. But the food was awful: a bit of salt goose that was almost too tough to eat, with sauerkraut which was raw and mushrooms pickled in a terrible, sharp acetic-acid vinegar. Afterward a cup of disgusting coffee made out of essence and a glass of fiery rum with a twang to it.

They went early to bed, but the tiny adjacent bedrooms under the roof were bitterly cold in spite of oil heating stoves. They could hear each other moving through the matchboard partition; the beds creaked at every movement. Alamein got into bed with her toes and fingers numb and could feel the cold creeping up her and her head almost frozen on the pillow. When she moved she could hear Amadeo muttering, and when he moved she said to herself:

"Why can't he lie quiet? If he's so restless he might come into bed with me and keep me warm. Even if he is a homosexual, he could do that."

At last she fell into a coma rather than asleep and in the early hours woke to find herself fully conscious but almost paralyzed. She felt like a marble woman inside her pajamas. At last she could hear people moving in the rooms below and got out of bed. The water in the jug was a block of ice. She called to Amadeo to get up. In the living room they crouched close to the central heating stove, swallowed some disgusting coffee, Amadeo paid, and they went on. They were both cold and exhausted, and Alamein began to pick a quarrel.

"I think that you behaved very badly to that nice Chinese professor. It was quite wrong to pretend that our car was being chased by rivals."

Amadeo began to laugh at the recollection.

"No, don't laugh. You in particular must never tell lies, otherwise nobody will believe that you are telling the truth when you say that you are going to build a city on the moon."

"I don't know that I am, or that anybody ever will build one."

"But you keep talking about it and you encourage Rollo to talk about it."

143

"He doesn't need much encouragement—and what is the harm? I really believe that it might be feasible. But you are a literal-minded child if you think that it is certainly possible or even likely."

"You oughtn't to say you can build a city on the moon when you don't know whether you can or not."

"Really, Alamein! You know as well as anyone that even if I get the millions of money necessary to make the attempt, my ideas may turn out to be unworkable."

"If you think they will be unworkable you oughtn't to claim that you can do it."

"I don't think they are unworkable. I think they are feasible but no one can be sure before they are tested. Besides, if I don't claim that I can build this imaginary city I shall never get the chance to try."

"In that case you are no better than Rollo. You are just another advertising man, putting business first, and not a scientist at all."

"What the hell is the matter with you this morning, Alamein?"

"So it is becoming personal! You think there is something the matter with me—or you pretend to think so—because I say that I shall never believe any of your wonderful claims again."

"You aren't always so childish," said Amadeo.

"You are perfectly intolerable, and you have been ever since Winston came to Geneva."

"What in Christ's name has Winston got to do with it?" asked Amadeo.

Alamein did not reply. She turned her head away and pretended to be asleep. Amadeo was upset and angry at her sudden attack. He was not certain that she might not after all be right—or partly right. Even if she was not, it was terrible that she should feel like that about him.

144

Probably his standards had become corrupted since working with Telefactors Ltd. But it was hard that Alamein, who had decoyed him into a partnership with Rollo, should now be upbraiding him for the inevitable results of that association.

Amadeo thought over the silly quarrel, without realizing that it was silly, until they were entering Berri.

Then Alamein, who had not said a word, asked to be put down where the drive to the château left the highway.

"You can bring my suitcase round later. I would rather arrive alone."

Alamein's tone was that of a princess giving orders to a groom, and if Amadeo had been an ordinary man he would have thrown her valise into the muddy lane. Suddenly she saw that she had made him unhappy; she had scored a victory. Her spirits rose.

As she walked down the drive to the point where she could see the lovely house standing back behind the pasture and the ha-ha, flanked by its great beech trees, she felt sudden pleasure and excitement. This place was where she belonged; here she would find the familiar faces that she loved. She stopped to look and savor the full beauty of the place before bursting in on them.

It was a windless cold morning, with weak sunshine. Patches of hoarfrost still showed in the shadows. Mounds of dead leaves lay heaped beside the drive where they had fallen or the wind had blown them. Yet here and there leaves were still hanging and the green of honeysuckle and ivy stood out. All was silent. All was the mirror of peace, that peace which steals out when man is absent from his haunts.

Alamein looked about. On a morning such as this, she had often seen a wakeful red squirrel searching for his hidden hoard. But there was no squirrel stirring. There

145

was not even a party of long-tailed tits hurrying from one network of twigs to the next. There was nothing. Feeling happy as she had not been for a long time, she walked up to the house.

To her surprise she was greeted by Pasionaria.

"Darling Alamein. I've lost my job. Such an emotional saga. I will tell you all about it later on. And you have just missed such an excitement. I had gone round to our uncle's to take him a bag of walnuts, and suddenly Lady Tonson descended on us in a grand car. She had come to talk to our uncle about Sir Sam's health and went off with him into his office, leaving me to do the honors. The man went off round the town for a stroll—rather rude I thought it. I remembered that we were having hare, so that there was enough food. I invited them to lunch here, and they came, and you can just imagine how Father enjoyed it. Of course he told us impossible stories about Diaghilev and invented a lot of completely new ones about Gertrude Stein. I didn't like Lady Tonson, Lady Billy, one bit. She is beautiful: one of those tall lean women with gold-brown hair. All nerves and whipcord. And her companion turned out to be a cook."

Leela came out, embraced her, and told her that lunch would be ready in five minutes.

At lunch Pasionaria and Leela were eager to tear Lady Tonson to pieces.

"That man with her was certainly her lover. One is always reading in novels about men sleeping with their cooks. Here is a woman who does."

"She was frightfully jealous because all his ears and eyes were for Pash," said Leela.

"Pash could have taken him away like that," she added, snapping her fingers.

146

St. Clair, who had greeted Alamein with an air of saddened affection, now intervened.

"No more scandal, you two women. You have no idea what an ill-considered word may do. During the war we all learned that a careless word might cost thousands of lives. But you two don't realize that in time of peace an ill-natured word may inflict torture on the innocent."

Leela found she could not take this.

"Listen to the damned old hypocrite! You say terrible things all the time, St. Clair."

"Yes, Leela. I am often to blame. I get carried away by my love of truth," he replied humbly.

"Come off it, Daddy," said Alamein. "I didn't come home to hear about your love of the truth."

St. Clair brushed this aside.

"During the last war I was a past master of careless talk. It once occurred to me to denounce a very pernicious local commander of the Hitler S.S. for running a protection racket for operators in the black market in his area in occupied France. I mentioned him by name, described his habits, and gave details and figures of his extortions. Well—a week later the fellow shot himself. I never knew whether he was innocent of what I had accused him of, but an inquiry had been ordered by his superiors and he could not face it."

Alamein knew that on this occasion St. Clair was telling the truth. When he embroidered there was a difference, and she could tell at once.

Next morning a filling came out of a tooth while Alamein was having breakfast, and she was in agony. Her first thought was to rush round to her uncle's. But when she called she learned that he would be out until the evening.

It would mean going to Paris. She would have to bear the pain until then. She called the family dentist.

"I can't fix a time, because his day is booked up. But there may be a cancellation, and in any case Monsieur Dupont will fit you in." It was the secretary of the dentist to whom she had been twice every year while her mother was alive—and who was still, in her mind, the only possible dentist in the world.

The pain was frightful. Alamein took the early train to Paris, which got her in soon after midday. At the dentist's she was half promised an appointment at half past three. With her face wrapped in a shawl, she wandered out into the street. It began to rain while she was in the Rue du Faubourg St.-Honoré, and she went to the first café she could see. She took refuge in the corner and ordered coffee and a *fine*. For a little while the intensity of the pain passed away, leaving only a dull ache, and she lifted her head.

There were some women sitting at tables in the room whom she took to be prostitutes. All of them were facing the door, whereas she had her back to it.

It interested her to study them: three gross women badly made up, with greasy fox furs, who might have been models for drawings by Toulouse-Lautrec. And then she noticed a tall girl who had just come in and from whose red plastic coat little rivulets trickled onto the floor. Her dark, highly colored painted face was wet also. There was a big mole in the middle of her right cheek: a *"grain de beauté"* which must be natural. But unlike the other women, she was beautiful, and there was a haughty look in her dark eyes when she noticed Alamein staring at her. But the haughtiness was superficial, like the polish on armor, and Alamein, still staring, saw that the girl was encased in armor which would preserve her from any

148

intimate contact and perhaps even from knowing herself what was inside it. Then, dropping her head again into her hands and staring not at the girl but at the pattern of the plastic tablecloth, Alamein asked herself if she too weren't wearing armor most of her life.

The whole value of human relationship, even of a life entirely alone, is the touch of naked protoplasm; offering oneself to experience, with no defenses, no anodyne, no drug of habit, nothing between the naked nerve and the object—whatever the object might be—lover, picture, poem, living animal, or the frosty air of winter and the night sky. Nothing else in the whole of one's life mattered, and here she was forfeiting it all in false defenses. That girl could not go on existing without armor: but she herself was encrusted absolutely unnecessarily.

And Alamein lifted her head to look again. A man was sitting at the table in front of the handsome thin girl. There was something familiar about him. After a moment they got up, a waiter opened a door opening onto a staircase, and they went up.

She had not been able to see the man's face, but she recognized him. He was her uncle. There could be no doubt: the shoulders, the stiff upright carriage, even the raincoat. Suddenly the pain came back; Alamein dropped her head and for a little while she could attend to nothing else. When the wave of pain had passed, she saw that it was almost time for the dentist, and, calling the waiter, paid her bill and went out into the rain.

She did not think about what she had seen until, with a temporary filling in her tooth, she was sitting in the train on the way home. For some reason which she could not understand, Alamein felt frightened by what she had discovered. It was not horrible; it was not disgusting; she was not shocked. But she wanted to cry, to crawl away and hide. Because it was Uncle Mathieu, whom she loved; and she suddenly realized how empty of love his life must have been with Fidèle. And that he, with his sensitive intelligence, should be driven to picking up a whore on a wet afternoon was so far, so far, from how life should have treated him. No wonder he had talked to her about a double standard of behavior and the demands of the gametes.

She would never be able to tell him, and yet if she did not her secret knowledge would come between them.

By the time she had got back to the Château de Berri, she was beginning to wonder if she could possibly be mistaken. She called his office, and in a little while Aunt Fidèle answered.

"The doctor had to attend a medical conference in Paris. I am expecting him back at any time now."

While they were sitting together after supper, with St. Clair apparently not listening but busy over the crossword, Leela asked:

"Do you have any little troubles in driving your droshky with the two horses, Alamein?"

"What droshky, what horses are you hinting at?"

"Don't be such an innocent, my pet, as Rollo would say if he were here," said Pasionaria. "You know perfectly well: the two in hand you have undertaken to drive like Phaëthon to the moon."

"Phaëthon was the charioteer of the sun," said Alamein.

"Don't try and sidestep Leela's perfectly fair question," said Pasionaria.

"What is it then?" asked Alamein.

"How do you manage two men who are madly in love with you?" asked Leela.

"But they are not," said Alamein. Then, seeing that

150

she was telling too much, she added hastily: "Of course Rollo may be; he's my husband. But Amadeo is completely sexless, like an angel. That's why I like him so much. But I never attempt to control either of them. I never talk to Rollo about Amadeo or to Amadeo about Rollo."

"Very wise of you," said St. Clair unexpectedly. Then he opened his mouth widely and said: "When I was still a moderately attractive young man I shared a flat with the two most notorious Sapphists of what I may call the Jix period. I shall disguise them under the names of Hengist and Horsa. Both of them, I need scarcely say, were madly in love with me. But not a word was spoken. I was a very promiscuous young man, and, as you may imagine, I lived with them in the most satisfying amity until I made what I thought was an innocent remark, but which turned out to be a very foolish one. I said: 'How happy we three are living like this together.' The result was that I was immediately chased out of the house. It was unfortunate for me, because I was very hard up at the time."

St. Clair seemed pleased with the impression he had made, picked up *The Times,* with its unsolved crossword, and went off to his own room. Leela followed him.

"He made that one up," said Pasionaria. "I saw him open his mouth before he began telling it."

Then she crossed the room and took her sister by both hands and said: "You were quite right to put Leela off, because she simply can't be trusted and she is such a fool. She simply doesn't understand about men being queer. She imagines that Amadeo has always been madly in love with you. And although Winston and she are so thick, she has never tumbled to his being a queer and to Amadeo

151

being in love with him. But I do wish you would confide in me."

"What do you want me to confide?" asked Alamein.

"Darling, don't try to be so innocent. About what you feel about Winston and Amadeo—and also how do you and Rollo and Amadeo get on *à trois?*"

Alamein looked at her sister steadily and, speaking in a very low voice, hardly above a whisper, said:

"I go to bed with both of them."

"Oh, how can you?" exclaimed Pasionaria, fascinated and horror-stricken.

"I need more than one man," said Alamein. Then, still looking Pasionaria in the eyes, she added:

"It is a blessing that Amadeo is there. Otherwise it might have been *anyone.*"

"But what you are telling me is horrible," said Pasionaria. "I don't understand how you can."

"You asked me to confide in you. And I have, because I can trust you, Pash, never to tell anyone."

"Of course you can trust me. But it is awful. I can't believe you would do that sort of thing." Pasionaria was flushed with excitement and avid for more.

"Of course, there is a reason for it. But I cannot tell you any more just now," said Alamein, and got up.

"Probably I ought not to have told you, because it is Amadeo's secret too. Good night, darling." And she went to her room. "St. Clair ought to be proud of me. I'm not his daughter for nothing," she said to herself. "Serve that nosy sister of mine right." All that night Alamein could not get to sleep. At first she lay rejoicing in her practical joke. Then she began to ask herself what she really felt and what she really wanted. Leela, with her words "two men who are madly in love with you," and her own crazy joke about going to bed with both Rollo and Amadeo had broken a bubble of illusion which had distorted her vision of herself. She did not love Rollo. He had imposed on her; she had imposed on herself. But she had only been pretending, and Amadeo had always been what mattered to her. She had dragged him into this silly company and to Geneva and had involved herself in marriage thinking that it would help him. It was all for his sake. Now she knew that he was a queer and that he loved her brother. What a mess. But if Amadeo liked her to be around, and he had seemed to while they were laying up his boat, and if she could be tactful and efface herself, they might accept her and they might all three be very happy together if she could learn to live without sex or jealousy. Other women had done it. It ought to be possible.

Well whatever happened she would never go to bed or live with Rollo again. She must tell him the truth as soon as she saw him. Writing was no good and would produce endless argument. A clean break must be by word of mouth.

Amadeo had gone to Paris and thence to London on some business with Sir Sam. She had a week alone with her family, and was amused to notice that Pasionaria kept out of her way. She seemed to have frightened her off asking for more confidences. It was as well that she had cleared her mind about Rollo, for it saved her worrying over a letter that arrived from Monsieur Plotz and which she did not bother to understand.

It ran as follows:

To M. Amadeo Severin
Copy to Madame Kitson
Sir,

As you are aware from our last conversation Telefactors Ltd. is overdrawn to the amount of 48,763

Swiss francs. There are current expenses rent and salaries of about 2,700 Swiss francs a month. In addition there are outstanding payments due to the subcontractors on the Formosan contract amounting to 111,230 Swiss francs which must be met within the next two months. These payments will increase rapidly during the coming year.

In this connection I must point out once more that there are 110,490 Swiss francs owing from M. Beaumont for the shares allotted to him on the formation of the company. But even if this were paid immediately, a financial reconstruction will soon be inevitable.

M. Kitson has cabled that he has already interested an American corporation in Telefactors and that they may be prepared to put up a really substantial amount of capital on condition that the existing shares are written down to 50% of their face value. He assures me that a majority of the shareholders will agree, and I have made representations to the bank on that understanding, and provided this is agreed, they are prepared to extend their cover until the American corporation has taken over, or for six months. They insist however that M. Beaumont's shares should be paid for in full before extending their cover.

Yours faithfully,
Hermann Egon Marie Plotz

Taking the letter in her hand, Alamein went into St. Clair's room at a time when he should have been writing but was still busy over *The Times* crossword.

"Darling Daddy, the Geneva bank is getting hysterical because you have not yet paid for the shares that were allotted to you. Telefactors S.A. appears to be overdrawn, because Rollo went off with our bank balance to America and there are some terrific bills to be paid. So they are asking you for about 111,000 Swiss francs so that we can carry on until Rollo comes back with American money."

"Oh no. You cannot ask me for anything like that. I have always given you everything you wanted, but I cannot give you everything that a bank clerk in Geneva may happen to want. You are well provided for by your mother—a provision that I have never questioned. But it is no good asking me for the moon or for the money to go there. That is not reasonable. Even a child like you should know that."

"No, Daddy, I'm not asking that. Indeed I'm not asking for anything myself. I don't mind whether you pay or not. But Rollo and the horrible man at the bank insist that you promised to take up 10,000 pounds' worth of shares in Telefactors and that you have only paid 700 and something. The shares have been allotted to you, and they say you owe them £9,240."

St. Clair shook his head gloomily.

"Ten thousand was, in round figures, an expression of my intentions and of my good will. From me that ought to have been enough. But I will look into it. My belief is that I have paid in full. But I cannot tell you now. I have a chapter to write. But I will look into it, my love, and if there has been an error on my part I promise you that I shall set it right."

St. Clair smiled and kissed her, holding her close for a moment, and Alamein went out of the room saying to herself that she had done all that she could and what did it matter anyway?

From now on she was going to have a rest from thinking about money. She had forgotten to show St. Clair Monsieur Plotz's letter with all the rigmarole about the Americans and writing down shares, whatever that signified. But it wasn't worth bothering about. No doubt it would all sort itself out. And if it didn't, the sooner that Telefactors went bankrupt the better. Rollo would go off after something else, and she might be useful to Amadeo in some other way. She was ready to do anything for him, but she hoped it would be sailing the boat or cooking or washing his shirts, and not being the director of a company.

A week passed by, then, without warning, Amadeo was back from London and was calling up from the terrace to the window of her room. She went to the garden door. It was a brilliant day of February sunshine: clear and actually warm. Amadeo looked very young and rather severe. There was something on his mind.

"Put on a coat and some outdoor shoes and come along for a walk. We can talk better out of doors." She pulled on some high boots and a sheepskin coat, then, with her heart beating hard, hurried out to where he was waiting. There was something different about Amadeo.

He did not speak until they were some distance from the château and were in the wood.

"Have you noticed anything peculiar about Pash?" he asked.

"What do you mean?"

"She seems to have gone mad. Dementia praecox or something. Uncle is wondering what he ought to do. And I had to come to tell you because it concerns us both."

"What is it?"

"Well, she went to Yseult and told her that you were a nymphomaniac and habitually went to bed with me as well as with Rollo. And she asked Yseult to tell Uncle so that he could do something about it. He believed the story, and this morning he told me that he congratulated me, but he thought I ought to know that we were being talked about."

Alamein had blushed as he spoke. Suddenly she said:

"It's all my fault. I told Pash. It was a joke. She was so foul about you and Winston, and I thought I would give her something to think about and shut her up. I never dreamed she would run round telling people and that they would believe it."

"You thought it was a joke," said Amadeo in icy tones.

Alamein said nothing. She felt the tears coming and bit her lips.

"Rollo won't think it a joke when he hears about it," he went on. "He'll certainly believe it is true whatever you say, or I say."

"Damn Rollo. I don't care what he believes." And Alamein burst into tears.

"It is you who are mad, not Pash. Aren't you ashamed of yourself? Do you still think it's a joke? What on earth possessed you to tell such a lie?"

"I suppose that I wished it were true," said Alamein, trying to swallow down her tears and glaring at him. Then she could not bear it any longer and turned and ran indoors and locked herself in her room.

"Oh, if I could kill myself, if I could hang myself," she muttered, searching for a piece of cord. There was a thin leather dog leash with a loop at one end. She slipped it round her neck and was standing on a chair trying to hook the swivel onto a picture nail above her head when there was a tap at the door. She got down, took off the noose, and, still holding the dog lead in one hand, unlocked the door. Amadeo was standing outside.

"Go away," she said.

"Did you mean what you said just now?"

157

"I don't know what you are saying," she replied.

"That you wished that we had been lovers."

"Why do you torture me? Of course it's true. Now go away."

She made a movement to shut the door, but Amadeo pushed her into the room and slammed the door. Then he caught hold of her and said: "If this is another joke, I shall never speak to you again."

"I was just going to hang myself with this," she said, showing him the dog leash. "Do you think the nail in the wall would have held?"

Amadeo took the leash out of her hand, opened the window, and threw it onto the terrace. He was kissing Alamein when the door opened and Leela stood in the entrance.

"I beg your pardon!" she exclaimed, and turned and bolted downstairs like a frightened rabbit.

"It is going to be awfully difficult to explain," said Alamein happily, some time later.

"Better not try. We shall only make things more complicated," said Amadeo.

"You'll have to explain to Uncle. We can't have him putting Pash into a loony bin," said Alamein. They began to laugh and found they could not stop. At last Amadeo said:

"I still don't see what made you tell that lie."

"I told you. Pash was so foul, always rubbing in that you are a queer and that you are in love with Winston. I wanted to shut her up, and thought I would do it properly."

"Me in love with Winston! Jesus Christ Almighty. What horrible creatures women are. Anyone who can imagine that I'm in love with Winston ought to be in a loony bin." Then, looking at Alamein and seeing something in her

158

face, he continued angrily: "You didn't believe anything so completely cuckoo? You don't mean to tell me . . . Did you believe I'm a queer?"

"Well, Pash talked about it as though she knew. She is awfully good at guessing things one wants to keep dark," said Alamein.

"So you believed her. You think I'm a queer too?"

Alamein put her arm round him. "Well, yes. Aren't you just a bit? You were so neutral. All that time on the boat you never made the faintest sign. You never touched me if you could help it."

"You had only just married Rollo. It would have been an impossible situation, and not fair on you. But to think that Winston and I . . ."

"Well you seemed so fond of him and took him to live with you on the boat."

"Only because the wretched boy was almost off his head, and Rollo and you would not do anything for him. So I had to." There was a silence. Then Amadeo asked:

"Was that why you suddenly stopped coming to the boat?"

"I wasn't wanted. I could see that."

"As a matter of fact, it was an awful strain when both you and Winston were on the boat. I was almost at breaking point. When you and I were alone together I was perfectly happy most of the time. Seeing you and sailing with you were almost enough."

"I have been feeling just like that. I have been saying to myself that it doesn't matter you being queer so long as you let me be with you. I can be happy cooking for you and washing your clothes."

Amadeo put his hands on her shoulders. "Don't say anything more. Don't make me cry. What a pair of fools."

"I tried to suppress how much I wanted you. I suppose

that's why it came out when I told Pash that I was always going to bed with you."

"It was clever of you. Otherwise we shouldn't have found out."

The bell for lunch was being rung downstairs.

"We had better tidy ourselves and go down. Promise that you'll stay for lunch."

"Yes, I'll stay. I am as hungry as a wolf."

"I feel a bit sick with emotion and with laughing."

"What have you two been up to? Some damned secret you won't tell us about, I suppose," said St. Clair. It was clear that neither Pash nor Leela had confided in him. "Well, out with it."

Amadeo put his finger to his lips and said "Hush!" and Alamein began to giggle. St. Clair shrugged his shoulders and began to talk about secrets that were kept during the war. Pasionaria was silent throughout the meal and did not look at either of the guilty parties.

7

Rollo cabled from the United States that he was returning and asked Alamein to meet him at Geneva airport, but she replied that she was staying at the Château de Berri and that Amadeo and she wished him to come there. He could discuss the difficulties with St. Clair.

He arrived just as they were sitting down to lunch, having driven from Geneva to Chatillon-sur-Seine the previous afternoon and evening.

He was in a bad temper and obviously annoyed at having had to drive all the way from Switzerland immediately after his arrival. Directly lunch was over he said: "We'll waive the coffee, Mr. de Beaumont, if you don't mind. I want to have a talk with you, and the sooner the better."

If St. Clair was surprised he did not show it, but brushed up his mustache, smiled, and said: "Come along, my dear boy. We have much to talk about."

Rollo took a chair in St. Clair's writing room and without even feeling for his pipe came straight to the point.

"Sir, on your verbal promise to take up 10,000 one-pound shares, which were afterward transformed to shares of twenty-five Swiss francs, which makes it roughly 5,000 shares, that number were allotted to you on the formation of the company. But you have only paid for an insignificant number of them. I was naturally most reluctant to press you, since you are my father-in-law. But the bank can no longer wait."

St. Clair wagged his head with amusement. "Banks always wait, my boy. They make all their money on overdrafts."

Rollo interrupted sharply. "You definitely told me you would take up the shares. I remember you said 10,000 shares allotted to you would look well in the prospectus. It is a matter of honor."

"If you think that the honor of St. Clair de Beaumont can be compromised by a Swiss bank clerk, you have a lot to learn."

"Do you deny that you promised to put up £10,000?"

"The figure of 10,000 is certainly correct. It is a noble figure, a round figure, which expressed my intentions and my good will. It was like me to have suggested it."

"Well, write a check then. Make it out for £9,240 to Telefactors Société Anonyme," said Rollo savagely.

St. Clair gazed at him in astonishment. "But, my dear fellow. I had all this out with Alamein, and as a result I searched through my accounts and I discovered that I had already paid you for your shares."

"We certainly have not received the money," said Rollo.

"I can show you the counterfoil," and St. Clair extracted a bunch of keys from his hip pocket and unlocked a drawer in his table and produced a little bright-pink checkbook—issued by the Société Générale.

"Here we are, my boy. Here you are: 10,000 payable to Telefactors S.A. on the 20th of August."

Rollo took the checkbook out of St. Clair's hands and looked at it, puzzled. Suddenly he said: "But that payment is in francs."

"New francs, mind you—not old ones," said St. Clair triumphantly. "You see, you were mistaken."

Rollo had recovered himself and said with fury:

"You know as well as I do that your promise was in pounds. I drew up that prospectus estimating the expenses of floating the company in pounds. Your promise was in pounds, and I shall hold you to it. I always calculate in pounds."

St. Clair looked at him with an expression of pity.

"That is a very rash thing to do, my dear boy. I am told that the pound will very probably be devalued."

Rollo knew he was beaten. He would like to have struck the older man, but turned away. "You will hear from my solicitors," he muttered as he went out of the door, though he knew it was a foolish thing to say. He would have knocked down anyone who stood in his path. He went savagely down the stairs, saying: "The bloody crook. The damned twister. Of course I never noticed he had paid 10,000 French francs, because they were credited as Swiss and it would have been a smaller figure. It is his word against mine, and he will get away with it." Such were his thoughts as he came to the bottom of the staircase and began to walk across the terrace, where to his surprise a group of people was standing. He had scarcely time to notice that one of them was Felix Hotchkiss, the man who had been his fellow guest at Les Oursins, and that Amadeo was driving up to them in his little car and was about twenty yards away when there was an explosion: the car stopped as though it had hit an invisible obstruction, and it was in flames. Before any of the watching group moved, Rollo had dashed across the terrace to his own car, snatched a fire extinguisher from under the seat, and was sprinting the few yards down the drive to the burning car. By that time Lady Billy, Alamein, and Doctor Robert were close behind him. As they reached him, he had smashed the window and was sweeping the flames away. Lady Billy pulled open the door and, with Rollo keeping the flames away, she and Alamein began to drag out Amadeo, who had sprawled forward unconscious, having cut his forehead on the windshield. He was difficult to get out; his ankle had jammed under the brake pedal. Once they had pulled him clear, they dropped him on the grass. Then when Rollo was satisfied that all the flames were extinguished, he helped them carry Amadeo to the house. Their burden recovered consciousness before they got there. But his attempt to stand up was unsuccessful, and he was helped into a chair that Felix carried out from the dining room, although there were several garden seats on the terrace.

Leela brought out a basin of water and a towel, and Doctor Robert sponged away the blood on his nephew's forehead.

"Nothing much. A cut on the hairline. Sticking plaster will be as good as a bandage. But he is scorched and shocked. If you people will clear away, I'll drive him back to my house and put him to bed. He'll be all right tomorrow. You'll have to postpone your meeting till then," said the doctor while he snipped away bloodstained locks of hair.

"Rollo is the hero of the hour," boomed St. Clair, who appeared carrying a bottle. There was a loud pop as a champagne cork flew skyward.

"A glass of champagne all round is what I prescribe, and Mathieu will endorse it." He filled glasses, but when it came to the turn of Amadeo, the chair was empty: Mathieu and Alamein had put him into the doctor's car and all three had driven off.

164

"I give you the health of that noble fellow Rollo Kitson —and to the speedy recovery of Amadeo Severin, who owes his life to the presence of mind and quickness of his partner. It is a fine thing to have a soldier in the family."

"I seem to have cut my wrist. Will you come and tie it up for me?" said Rollo to Pasionaria. They went up to the bathroom amid the hubbub of discussion as to what exactly had happened and why it had, with Rollo shaking off greetings and congratulations.

To Pasionaria the big man with his bleeding wrist (Rollo had been cut by broken glass from the window of the car) seemed to be a different order of being from the wretched cook and two women who had arrived unexpectedly with Lady Billy Tonson.

In the bathroom she washed his wound, swabbed it, and bound it up with a narrow bandage. Occasionally she looked up at him with her eyes glowing with worship.

"It is what you would do—to save *him*," she whispered.

From her tone Rollo realized that "there was something cooking." But he did not immediately ask a question. He was himself suffering from shock—a shock of surprise. And he resented that old crook calling him a hero and toasting him in champagne only ten minutes after defrauding him of £9,000. So he said: "Look here, Pash. I am longing for a drink, but let's have it up here. I don't want all that hoo-ha. So see if you can swipe a bottle and a couple of glasses."

"Come into my room—we shall be safe from any of those women coming up to use the loo," said Pasionaria.

Rollo sat in her bedroom only vaguely taking in photographs and china cats and an achievement of the Du Bartas coat of arms which would have told a more ob-

165

servant man something about the character of its occupant.

Then Pasionaria returned with a bottle of brandy and wineglasses. He drank off what she poured, and she refilled his glass. Rollo sat on an armchair and she facing him on the bed.

Then she said very seriously: "I do admire you, Rollo. You show such wonderful dignity and restraint, and I feel so ashamed of Alamein. . . ." She paused, but Rollo remained silent.

"I think her going off just now with Amadeo—in front of everybody—it was so brazen. . . ."

Rollo made an impatient movement, seemed about to speak, but thought better of it and subsided, waiting for the next thing she would say.

"Whatever one thinks about marriage . . . it is so cruel after only a few months. . . . I want to say I feel so bitterly sorry that it has turned out this way. . . ."

"Are you telling me that Alamein is having an affair with Amadeo?" said Rollo quietly.

"Oh my God! But I understood you knew all about it. What have I done!" exclaimed Pasionaria in tones of horror.

Rollo jumped up from his chair; she from the bed and seized him by the arms. "Don't go. I won't let you go until you promise not to do anything rash. . . . In front of all these people." Then, clinging to Rollo's shoulders and letting her head fall on his chest, she burst into tears. Rollo held her tight; he kissed her; then he freed one arm and poured out some more brandy and drank it off. Then he sat down with her on the bed, still with his arm round her shoulders. She nestled close to him and sobbed at intervals.

"What evidence have you, Pash, for what you've said?"

166

"I shall never be able to face seeing Alamein again. I've betrayed her confidence."

"It's just as well that you have. It couldn't be concealed for long, Pash." And Rollo kissed her again and held her very close. "You had better tell me the whole thing now."

"It was so horrible. She boasted about it. She said she was going to bed with both of you," Pasionaria managed to get out between her convulsive sobs.

"She told you that! By God. I still can't quite believe it. While she was going with him on the boat. What a bloody little bitch."

"Somehow I thought from the way she said it that you knew. That she wasn't troubling to conceal it. Oh, how horrible." Pasionaria broke down, and the tears trickled down her cheeks into her mouth, so that Rollo tasted the salt, and that and her convulsive movements of misery excited him.

"Here, drink some of this," he said, putting the glass of brandy to her lips. She took a gulp. He finished the glass and poured himself some more.

Rollo removed his arm from her shoulders, even edged away from her a little way along the bed, and sat, his head bowed in thought. It had occurred to him that anything he said to Amadeo, or to Alamein, about their affair was bound to jeopardize the proposals he had to put forward at the meeting tomorrow—that is, if Amadeo was well enough. Whatever he was going to say—a divorce perhaps was the most rational—whatever he decided would have to wait. And the idea that everything he had fixed up in New York might come to nothing because that little bitch he had married wanted to play about with two men made him much angrier than the fact of her infidelity in itself.

Pasionaria had recovered herself and was watching him uneasily while he sat, his head bowed forward, apparently unconscious of her presence.

"I've always loved you, Rollo. I would do anything in the world to help."

"Well, promise me you won't say a word; won't let Alamein guess that you've told me." He turned on her savagely. "If you show in any way what's happened, that there is anything out of the ordinary—well, I'll—I'll never speak to you again. Promise me. Promise me, Pash, if you really do love me."

She nodded, fell into his arms, and a long, long embrace sealed the promise and then another one, and Rollo found himself lying beside her and undoing her clothes.

Pasionaria roused herself from her mood of deep emotional acquiescence to get out of bed and say: "I'll lock the door." And having locked it she was back again in her deep dream state, lying with more clothes discarded to await his will.

Rollo was reflecting: "A damned good revenge on that bitch Alamein, and this ought to help keep Pash's mouth shut." Then he went to it.

Rollo and Pasionaria saw no one when they went downstairs, and Rollo drove off. He was a man who hated being alone: it was always difficult for him to part from his last companion and he would have liked to have taken Pash with him, at all events for dinner. But it was essential to get the meeting over and the proposals accepted before having it out with Alamein. If he went off with Pash to Paris or to some other town it would arouse comment. So, regretfully, he got into his car and drove off alone.

———

While this had been going on at the château, Alamein had been waiting in her uncle's office. She wanted to talk to him alone, but there were several patients, and it was two hours before the last one had gone and Mathieu came out and saw her.

"Still waiting? There's nothing to worry about. I gave him a pretty strong sleeping pill. He'll be all right when he wakes up. There is nothing that can't wait, my little tart. Or have you gone back to being a hart's-tongue fern?"

"You remember that talk we had about ferns and things?" asked Alamein.

"Of course I do."

"Well you went on to say that businessmen have two codes of behavior. But Rollo has only got one. Everything is business. Everything he does is done for the sake of something else: not for its own sake. All his motives are ulterior motives."

"Most of us have rather mixed motives for what we do," said her uncle. "And usually we don't know what they are."

"Well that's not true of Rollo. He has everything planned out. All his charm, all his love, all his camaraderie, is planned and has to produce its dividend. I tell you that I have found out about him."

"You don't make him sound like a human being," said her uncle.

"He is only completely a human being when he loses his temper. It is as though a bad temper were his only genuine quality."

There was an interval. Alamein waited for her uncle to say something, but he remained silent.

"People find his qualities which aren't genuine very charming," she added.

169

"You must have done when you married him."

"Yes. But I was acting from an ulterior motive too. I married him to help Amadeo. And he married me for the same reason: to get hold of Amadeo. I suppose there is nothing to choose between us."

"There was no ulterior motive when he put out the fire and saved Amadeo's life. Give him credit for courage and quickness and sense."

"Yes. I do. That was the real man. One sees it when he loses his temper."

"Have you finished with him?" Alamein nodded her head and went back to the château.

The meeting was held next morning in the dining room of the Château de Berri. All except two of the shareholders were present. Rollo was the chairman and rose and addressed the meeting as follows:

"Ladies and Gentlemen. For reasons I shall not go into here in detail beyond saying that we have been let down in our legitimate expectations, we find ourselves in a desperate financial position. Before I went to New York I realized that there was need for the reconstruction of the company, and there is more urgent need now. Fortunately I was able to make contacts with a group which is deeply interested in our inventions. They are ready to put up very substantial sums. But of course they are businessmen, and after several stiff discussions I was forced to agree that the shares of the existing shareholders should be written down to half their nominal value. As you no doubt understand, this makes no difference whatever to their *real* value, which depends entirely on whether our inventions are taken up and we are able to sell licenses for the manufacture of our products."

"It does, however, affect our position relative to the newcomers," said Sir Sam.

"I was just coming to that," said Rollo. "Earl Shagreen becomes president. I become vice-president. My wife retires as a director. Amadeo Severin retires as a director and becomes technological adviser, which is indeed what he always has been."

Rollo looked round the room at the faces: some bored, some puzzled, some rather glum.

"Of course, we have to make sacrifices—but I will repeat they are really nominal ones. But we save the company and in future we can go ahead without—" and here Rollo looked at St. Clair—"without the financial worries that have bedeviled us up to now."

"The question is: Have they the resources that I need for further research? Are you sure they will provide that?" asked Amadeo.

"Well, you know that your demands may go up and up. I can't promise astronomic sums. But they realize that research may be a major item in our budget."

St. Clair suddenly bestirred himself, and said: "Before we continue to discuss the future, I wish to ask Captain Kitson a question about the recent past—only yesterday. When you were then asking me, owing to an unfortunate misunderstanding, to pay for a block of shares which you had apparently allotted me, were you intending that they should be written down to fifty per cent of their value directly you had got my check in your pocket?"

"Those shares would have been treated exactly like all that were originally subscribed for and allotted. You could not expect exceptional treatment because you were behindhand in paying for them," said Rollo.

"That was a deliberate attempt to swindle me," growled

171

St. Clair. No one appeared to have heard the remark. Sympathy was with Rollo.

"Well, since I suppose that there is no alternative, I agree to joining with Mr. Shagreen and his associates," said Amadeo. He was bored and wanted to be quit of the whole thing and get on with finding out why his car had exploded.

"I'll put it to the vote. Those in favor . . ."

"Just a minute, Mr. Chairman," said Sir Sam. "I would like to have one or two things made crystal clear before this is put to the vote. With the writing down of the shares and the retirements from the board, control passes to the American company, doesn't it?"

"I regret it, but it is inevitable," said Rollo.

"And they take over the service agreements signed by yourself and Amadeo Severin?" asked Sir Sam.

"Naturally. Those agreements are the principal assets of the company. And of course they are our protection."

"So that they could direct Signor Severin's researches into whatever channels they liked for the next twenty years?" These words awoke a memory in Alamein.

"No doubt that is possible, but it is scarcely likely, since we are all dependent on his profound—shall I say gen?" said Rollo.

Alamein spoke up: "They could also, I suppose, put a restrictive covenant on all his future work in science?"

"They are scarcely likely to do that, because they are paying in order to be associated with him," replied Rollo.

"But it might happen if they sold Telefactors to the American government?"

"I suppose anything might happen if they were able to do that. But of course we should all be millionaires if they could bring that off—and not in old francs either," said Rollo, looking at St. Clair.

172

"It's rather a question of whether Amadeo wants to be a millionaire at the cost of giving up research," said Sir Sam.

"You seem to be forgetting that there is no alternative to these proposals. We are in a jam, and this is the only way out," said Rollo. His temper was only just under control.

"Well, Mr. Kitson seems to think that there is no alternative to writing down our shares and handing over to these Americans with the Sharkskin President. But I propose one which will leave Amadeo free to continue whatever research interests him, and that is that we wind up the company and go into voluntary liquidation," said Sir Sam.

"That means bankruptcy and that you lose everything that you have invested," said Rollo.

"Bankruptcy, possibly—but not loss. I am willing to take over the Formosan contract for a sum which will pay all debts and return their money in full to all the shareholders."

"You can't do that. I am committed to the American corporation."

"My offer would include a year's salary free of tax for Mr. Kitson. We do not wish to penalize him," said Sir Sam.

"The Formosan government would have to be consulted," said Rollo. But he had to admit that he had not consulted it about the American take-over.

The discussion continued with growing bitterness, but it was soon apparent that Sir Sam's proposal had won the day, and Rollo's was the only dissentient vote.

The meeting dispersed, and Alamein was alone with Rollo.

"Well, you bitched it up. I suppose you are pleased with yourself?"

"I ought to have told you before, but there wasn't an opportunity. I'm in love with Amadeo," said Alamein.

"No opportunity! You've been sleeping with him for months," said Rollo. His anger had gone cold on him, and he wanted to finish and to be free to plan for what could be saved. Alamein was a failure and a write-off, and he hated being confronted with her.

She looked surprised and then said: "So Pash has been telling tales."

"Yes. Pash has been telling tales."

Alamein gave a mirthless laugh, which was almost an exclamation of disgust, and shrugged her shoulders.

"You won't believe me, but there isn't a word of truth in what Pash has been telling you. I've no doubt she believes it. It's a silly story. . . . The truth is that Amadeo and I have only made love once, which was four days ago. I think I have always been in love with him, but it took a long time for me to find it out."

"And the only way was to marry me, I suppose?"

Alamein did not reply.

"I suppose it was always obvious, in a way. Well, I shan't be here to pull him out next time he sets himself on fire. A restrictive covenant is about all he is fit for."

There was another long pause. Alamein looked at the ground, twisting up her handkerchief and longing for the moment when Rollo would go.

"I did my best, and you've bitched it up properly." Rollo suddenly laughed. "But my God your father's a twister. You know, he paid his 10,000 in francs, not in pounds, and he actually boasted, 'New francs . . . not old ones.' That's where you get it. It's in your blood." He stopped, and said in a quite different tone:

174

"I wish things had worked out. I suppose you'll want a divorce. We had better keep in touch and fix that up."

And without the last embrace that Alamein had feared, he opened the door and walked out. A few moments later she heard his car start and looked out of the window. To her astonishment, Pash was sitting beside him.

While Rollo and Alamein had been talking and exchanging what were to prove their farewells, Lady Billy had said to St. Clair:

"I want to ask you to talk to my friend Felix Hotchkiss, and also to Roma Palgrave. Felix has an enormous admiration for Marcel Proust, and Sam tells me that you knew him intimately."

"Come into my room, dear people," and St. Clair led the way into his study.

"This is where I write my books. You see here the simple and perfect surroundings of an author who has never been content merely to repeat his successes."

Felix Hotchkiss brushed this opening—which was obviously likely to lead to a flood of self-revelation—firmly to one side.

"You actually knew Proust and were on very intimate terms with him. In fact, he was in love with you, wasn't he, when you were a very young man?" he asked.

"I don't know who told you that," said St. Clair. "I did know him and I didn't. I once spent an afternoon telling him about Henry James. I said he was much the greatest writer in the world, but Proust was bored, and when I thought about it afterward I realized that he probably hadn't been listening and that I had stayed too long." St. Clair paused, reflecting. "These meetings with the great when one is a young man are always disappointing. One generation cannot understand another.

And one is forever after thinking of what might have been. I was talking about Proust the other day—or a few months ago—it might have been to your husband, Lady Billy, and what I said brought back something I had completely forgotten. When I was first introduced to him, Proust told me that I looked like Rimbaud. That might have led to something—but at seventeen I had never heard of Rimbaud—much less read him. So you see I cannot be said to have known him intimately."

Leela called to them to come into the drawing room to have drinks. As they went in, they saw Rollo and Pash hurrying across the terrace and then driving away. A few moments later Alamein came into the room. She could think at that moment of only one thing and she would have liked to cry out to all the company:

"Rollo has gone and taken Pash with him!"

She could scarcely believe what she had seen. Surprise almost inhibited joy. Perhaps they had only gone into town to buy pipe tobacco! But in her heart she knew it was final. They were gone for good.

But she was not allowed to think about it or to realize it. Someone was saying: "I believe you and Amadeo love sailing, don't you? When the weather is a bit warmer perhaps you'll both come for a cruise on the *Connie?*"

And Alamein found herself accepting the invitation as though Amadeo and she were an old-established couple. She had not had time to look carefully at Lady Billy before: a tall slim woman with very blue eyes who looked straight into her own. One of her front teeth was filled with gold and kept catching the light; she had little, pointed eyeteeth. She was asking about sailing on the Lake of Geneva and she was dressed in tight black trousers with a black silk jersey that hung very flat in front. And her stomach was flat, like a boy's. Alamein found it difficult to talk and take in all these details. And at the same time she was wanting to cry out and tell everyone: "Rollo has gone and he has taken Pash with him!"

And then St. Clair was attracting everyone's attention and making an announcement—no, issuing an invitation. "It is Friday, and it is our custom for Mathieu to feast with us on Fridays. So we shall be expecting all of you here to dinner tonight. It is for me a very special day. I shall tell you all why tonight."

And with self-control that was unexpected by all his family, St. Clair said no more. Proust surveyed them all from his shoulder through half-closed eyes.

Felix had been helping Leela since the morning in planning the meal, and then in cooking it, and it was notable.

Each diner had a little terrine containing piping-hot minced cockscomb, sweetbread, and mushroom stewed in cream and decorated with slices of green olives. This was followed by roast pheasant, with braised celery, salad of *scarole* and matchstick potatoes. Small goat cheeses wrapped in chestnut leaves, with water biscuits and butter followed. Then the sweet—*Crème Brûlée*—after the cheese, in French fashion. A dessert of medlars, *marrons glacés*, and grapes concluded the meal.

The wine was Chambertin 1949, "old but still drinkable," said St. Clair modestly. Coffee and a very good brandy followed.

Conversation went like this.

"Do you really believe that you will build a city on the moon?" asked Lady Billy, turning to Amadeo.

"I doubt if I shall. But I think that some people will one day be making use of an improved version of my invention."

177

"Why should you doubt it?" asked Alamein, speaking across the table and neglecting Sir Sam, who was sitting beside her.

"It sounds improbable; after all, nobody has actually been there," said Lady Billy.

"I have no idea whether anyone will ever want to live in my city. I certainly would not. But that has nothing to do with the question of whether it is possible to build it."

"It is all too likely that the boy will succeed," said St. Clair. "Whatever man dreams of doing, he either does or believes he has done it. And whatever some men imagine turns out to be true."

"Who are you thinking of?" asked Dr. Robert, with a malicious twinkle in his eye.

"Oddly enough, Mathieu, I was at that moment thinking of Dean Swift, and not of myself," said St. Clair.

"Which of his imaginings has turned out to be true?" asked Sir Sam. "Tell us about it."

"Well, in *Gulliver's Travels* Swift tells us that the astronomers of Laputa have discovered two lesser stars, or satellites, which revolve about Mars; the innermost being distant from the center of the planet three of his diameters and the outermost five. The satellites of Mars were first discovered in 1877. One of them is so close to Mars that it revolves round the planet three times in one Martian day. The other so much farther that it takes two days between rising and setting and another two days between setting and rising. They are so small that it is very difficult to observe them, but Swift described them a hundred and fifty years before they were first seen."

A short silence fell on the company while they brooded on this.

"From something Dr. Robert said, I guess that you

have the same gift as Dean Swift," said Lady Billy. "Am I right?"

"I seemed to have it at one time," he answered gloomily.

"This is really exciting. Give us an example of your gift," said Lady Billy.

"I will, instead, tell you a story—the facts slightly changed, since I think it is certainly an official secret and I have no wish to be expelled from France or prosecuted in England. Well, I once put out a red herring. I gave a detailed account of how Himmler had arranged to brainwash the youth of France and bring them up as Germans of a lesser breed within the law—much as we British quite unconsciously brainwashed a selected number of Hindus and transformed them into old Harrovians, or the products of Sandhurst. I gave details of the plot, with the names of the châteaux where it was being carried on in youth camps, and of the French ministers and police officials who were implicated. I did this because the reverse was true. These camps were being run by French patriots, and my attack was planned to divert suspicion from them.

"Unfortunately one of my friends—the bravest man I have ever known—and I was a close friend of Lawrence of Arabia; I mention him not to boast, or to drop names, but to show you the standard of courage I am speaking of—my friend was an agent then in France, and he thought it would be valuable to collect evidence of the brainwashing. So at the risk of arrest and torture, he approached a police official who he thought was venial and offered him a very large sum of money for the full curriculum of the brainwashing establishment. He eventually got it and returned safely to England bringing his prize with him. He got a cool reception from his chiefs. Later on I was shown the book, in which the details of my red herring were expanded in a most ridiculous manner.

179

I could never enlighten him, of course. And yet, his book might just conceivably have been genuine."

Sir Sam was obviously fascinated by St. Clair. He was so eager that, though Dr. Robert had twice looked at his watch, no one had the heart to break up the conversation.

"Give us an instance of your second sight," asked Sir Sam.

St. Clair thought for a moment and then brushed up his mustache and said: "There was a perfectly foul Hun—an S.S. commander in northern France. I ventured on giving a biographical sketch of the man and said that while he was a student when he gave a party in his room he used to serve sandwiches which he made by smearing live flies on the jam so that his guests would eat flies without knowing what they were doing. I don't know why I said it. It just came to me. Well, that man was taken prisoner, and during his interrogation he asked: 'How did you know about those sandwiches? That story on the radio went all round and did me a lot of harm. It lost me promotion.'"

"You can't tell us why you thought of such an improbable and unpleasant thing?" asked Lady Billy. "Was it telepathy?"

"More likely some vague unconscious memory of Garibaldi biscuits," replied St. Clair sadly.

The company had forgotten St. Clair's promised announcement, but now he rapped on the table and said:

"You all know that I am a writer. I have written ten novels in English which have met with only moderate success except among such discerning lovers of literature as my guest here tonight, Sir Sam. Somewhere about two years ago I decided to write no more in English. I would see what I could do in French. After all, during the war my audiences had all been French or Belgian. I am equally at home in both languages, and the subject of the book I wished to write was of more importance to Frenchmen than to the lucky and perfidious inhabitants of Britain. Both subject and language inspired me, and I have never been so aware that the book I was writing was going to be a magnificent work of art. I am fully satisfied with my own work—a state of mind which is rarer than you would suppose."

"It requires genius of an uncommon order to be able to please oneself," said Mathieu.

"You are always ironical, my dear Mathieu," drawled St. Clair. "But on this occasion I have been able to please others besides myself, and today I received a telegram from my publisher to tell me that my novel, *La Victoire Infecte* has been awarded the Prix Goncourt."

When the congratulations had somewhat subsided, Mathieu said: "Show us the telegram."

"Really, Mathieu, you exceed the limits of polite behavior. If this dinner table is a court of law and I am a witness in the box, I must ask for the protection of the court in the person of Sir Sam if I am to be accused of perjury."

Alamein could see that both St. Clair and her uncle were angry and that it was time for a diversion. She therefore stood up, clapped her hands to attract the attention of the company, and said:

"It is the greatest and happiest of days, and we have all won prizes. My father has the Prix Goncourt, Amadeo is free, I also have got my freedom, and even the shareholders of Telefactors have got their money back. It is no time to quarrel over my uncle's jokes. So I ask you all to fill your glasses while I give you a toast."

Glasses were filled, and the company waited expectantly.

"To Pash and to Rollo—and may they be happy."

The toast was drunk amid a buzz of inquiries, some laughter, and the raising of some eyebrows, but it achieved its object—for the quarrel which had been on the point of breaking out went no further.

Sir Samuel and Lady Billy, Felix Hotchkiss and Mrs. Palgrave were all spending the night at the château, but the time came for Amadeo, Dr. Robert, and Yseult to go home. Amadeo went first, and Alamein accompanied him while Dr. Robert was looking for a mislaid muffler. It was cold outside, and the dark night blazed with stars. Facing them, in the southeast, Orion hung like a golden gridiron. Alamein and Amadeo walked as far as the ha-ha.

"I have never seen the stars so bright," said Amadeo.

And forgetting that her uncle and Yseult were coming up behind them, Alamein gripped his shoulder and drew him toward her. "*Qu'as-tu?*" he murmured, but she drew his head close and kissed him on the mouth. They stood like a dark pillar in the path, Alamein's silk dress gleaming a little in the starlight. They heard Mathieu say: "The Prix Goncourt! It's too much! I wish I knew whether it's true." Then without a word the old doctor and his daughter stepped round them and went on down the drive.

"She is advertising her relationship," said Yseult when they had reached their car and got into it.

"She is free to do as she likes. But we say nothing," said her father. "We won't wait. Amadeo can walk." They drove off. The two lovers clung together in an embrace which lasted a long time.

They looked up at the blazing stars. Orion was still there studded with gold. Their thoughts carried them for a moment into space beyond the sun and his planets, and they knew that nothing human mattered in that triumphant universe of infinite space and infinite time.

Then they looked down, trying to read each other's faces in the starlight, and they laughed.

"I was crazy to think that I loved anyone but you," said Alamein.

"Don't let's talk about it any more," said Amadeo.

"And it's crazy for you to go back to Mathieu's. Come back and spend the night in my room. I'll see if the coast is clear. Not that it matters."

So Amadeo went back with her into the château.